MANDIE®
AND THE
SEASIDE
RENDEZVOUS

DISCARD

Mandie® Mysteries

MANDIE®
AND THE
SEASIDE
RENDEZVOUS

Lois Gladys Leppard

BETHANY HOUSE PUBLISHERS
MINNEAPOLIS, MINNESOTA 55438

Published by Bethany House Publishers
A Ministry of Bethany Fellowship International
11400 Hampshire Avenue South
Minneapolis, Minnesota 55438
www.bethanyhouse.com

Printed in the United States of America by
Bethany Press International
Minneapolis, Minnesota 55438

ISBN 1-55661-673-2

For Andy Unseth,
without whom this book
wouldn't be.

and

With Thanks to

Mrs. Eddie-Joyce Geyer
St. Augustine Historical Society

and

Ms. Melissa Stuart
St. Augustine Lighthouse/Museum

For their aid in researching
this time period
of St. Augustine, Florida.

Contents

"Nothing is more heartbreaking
than to trust someone
who can't be trusted."

—Anonymous

Chapter 1 / Off to the Seaside

Mandie Shaw and her friend Celia Hamilton gazed in wonderment as they traveled through the beautiful seaside territory after the train left Jacksonville, Florida. Now and then they spotted the rippling ocean behind the huge dunes of glistening white sand. Clusters of palm trees waved their fronds in the wind. Sea gulls fluttered about as the noise of the train disturbed them.

"I smell the water!" Mandie declared, taking a deep breath as she leaned against the window.

Celia looked at her friend and asked, "But how can you smell it when all the windows are closed?"

"Because the doors at the ends of the cars are open," Mandie reminded her. She looked at her grandmother, who was sitting in the next seat.

Mrs. Taft smiled at her and said, "You may open the window one inch—just one inch, now. I don't want to blow away and get covered with dirt."

"Oh, thank you, Grandmother," Mandie said,

quickly grasping the window latch. "Here, Celia, get the latch on your side and I'll push on mine."

With Celia's help, the window slowly moved upward until Mandie decided it was an inch, and they stopped. The girls immediately knelt down on their seats and put their faces next to the opened window.

"Oh, now I can feel the sand in the air!" Mandie exclaimed, rubbing her hands together.

"And I can almost hear the roar of the ocean above the *clackety-clack* of the train," Celia said.

Mandie looked at her friend and asked, "Can't you almost taste the smell of the ocean?"

Celia frowned, took a deep breath, and replied, "Why, I believe I do."

At that moment Mandie's white cat, Snowball, who had been sleeping on the floor, rose, stretched, and jumped up into the seat with his mistress. He stood up on his hind paws as he reached up to the opened window.

Mandie smiled at him and said to Celia, "Even Snowball is interested in the ocean."

"I hope he's not interested in it enough to run off from Senator Morton's house while we're there. You know your grandmother said the senator lives near the ocean," Celia said.

Mandie glanced at her grandmother, who had her eyes closed and was either dozing or just resting and not wishing to be disturbed. Turning back to Celia, she said, "At least we're only going to be at his house for two weeks out of this year. 1902 is just flying by."

"Two weeks is long enough for you to find a mystery and solve it," Celia teased.

"I don't know what kind of a mystery we could find at Senator Morton's house," Mandie said. Then she lowered her voice, hoping her grandmother couldn't hear her over the noise of the train, and added, "I'm just wishing the time away until we can get back home and get together with Sallie and Jonathan and Joe, I hope. It'll be just terrible if Joe has to stay at college all summer. It will ruin our plans to visit each other's houses this summer."

"The rest of us could still go ahead with the plan," Celia told her.

The train gave a sudden lurch as it rounded a curve, and both girls sat down hard on their seats. Mrs. Taft straightened up and opened her eyes.

A uniformed attendant who was pushing a tea trolley entered their car, and Mrs. Taft beckoned to him. As he approached, she asked the girls, "Would y'all like tea or something?"

"Oh yes, ma'am," Mandie quickly replied as she watched the man and tried to see exactly what he had on the cart.

"So would I, Mrs. Taft, thank you," Celia said, also turning to inspect the contents of the trolley.

The man stopped in front of Mrs. Taft's seat and said, "Madam, we have hot tea, hot cocoa, hot coffee, and sweet biscuits." He waved his hand over the items on his cart.

"Tea, please," Mrs. Taft told him.

"Cocoa, please," both girls said at once.

"Thank you," the man said. He placed a lap tray on the empty seat beside Mrs. Taft, filled two cups with cocoa and one with tea, and set them on the tray with three sweet biscuits, each on a separate little china plate. Then fanning out three folded white linen napkins, he handed one to Mrs. Taft and the other two to the girls. "Is there anything else, madam?"

"No, thank you, this is fine," Mrs. Taft replied, reaching to pick up her cup of tea.

The girls watched the man go on down the aisle with his cart and then turned to get their cups of cocoa.

"This train is so much nicer than any I've ever been on," Mandie remarked, sipping the cocoa and looking around at the plush furnishings.

"Yes, I agree," Celia said, picking up her cup.

"I don't suppose either of you has ever been on this line," Mrs. Taft told them. "This is the Florida East Coast Railroad, and it was built for luxury to entice those wealthy northern people to come to Florida."

"And did it work?" Mandie asked.

"Yes. According to Senator Morton, his hometown, St. Augustine, has become a real tourist attraction," Mrs. Taft replied.

"Like New York?" Celia asked.

Mrs. Taft smiled and said, "Oh, nothing like that. St. Augustine is really just a small town, even though it is the oldest city in the United States."

"Well, since it's the oldest city in our country, I would expect everything to be old and worn out," Mandie told her, holding her cup with both hands as the motion of the train shook the contents. Snowball came to sit by her, hoping for food.

"Watch that cat, Amanda," Mrs. Taft told her. "Don't let him cause you to spill that cocoa. And no, everything in St. Augustine is not old and worn out. It's old, of course, but the architecture is beautiful and the buildings are well preserved."

"Does Senator Morton live alone?" Mandie asked as she settled down in her seat. "I mean, I know he doesn't have a wife."

"No, Senator Morton's wife died shortly after your grandfather Taft passed away, many years ago," Mrs. Taft explained. "Because your grandfather was also a senator, Senator Morton and I were close friends."

"Does he have children?" Celia inquired as she, too, sat down.

"They never had any children," Mrs. Taft replied. "Senator Morton has several servants who have been with him a long, long time. One of the servants, Pedro, was raised by Senator Morton and his wife. Pedro's parents were employed by the Mortons, and they were both killed suddenly in an accident when Pedro was a small child. Senator Morton has a kind heart and gives a home to people who are needy and would like to work."

"No children," Mandie repeated. Looking at Celia, she added, "Sounds like no fun."

"Amanda, there are probably some young people in his neighborhood and among his friends," Mrs. Taft told her. "I'm sure you'll find a way to have fun." She smiled at her granddaughter.

As the train finally came into the city of St. Augustine, the girls became excited. The town was indeed beautiful, with large, ornate buildings that had many fancy architectural curlicues. There were several landscaped parks with water fountains and benches. Lots of people, richly dressed, strolled about the streets as the train passed through.

Senator Morton was waiting for them at the train station. Mandie and Celia watched as he squeezed Mrs. Taft's hand when she stepped down onto the platform. The girls looked at each other and smiled.

Ever since they had met the senator, which was on the ship going to Europe during the previous summer, they had discussed the two grown-ups behind their backs. Their conclusion was that Senator Morton was in love with Mrs. Taft, but they never could decide about Mrs. Taft. Sometimes she seemed in love with the man, and other times she was only polite and friendly. This visit could turn out to be interesting after all, Mandie decided. At least she and Celia would have something to discuss.

After greetings were exchanged, Senator Morton led them to his carriage, which was parked nearby. Mandie held tightly to her white cat while the servants took care of their luggage. The short journey to his house was exciting as they passed by old houses, built of a strange-looking kind of stone and in shapes and sizes the girls had never seen before. The city was nothing like Mandie's hometown back in Franklin, North Carolina, with its greenery and rolling hills and mountains. St Augustine's streets were narrow, and the houses were built close together.

"Here we are," the senator spoke from the front seat beside Mrs. Taft.

The girls quickly looked ahead and gasped as the vehicle came to a halt in the yard of what looked to them like a castle. The senator helped Mrs. Taft alight from the carriage, and the girls followed.

"You live here?" Mandie asked as she gazed at the huge house and held tightly to Snowball.

"Oh, it's enormous," Celia said.

Senator Morton looked back at the girls and smiled as he led Mrs. Taft to the front door. "It's not really any larger than your grandmother's house in Asheville, North Carolina, Miss Amanda."

"It sure looks like it is," Mandie declared.

"That's because it has all the fancy trimming," the senator replied.

Suddenly a tall, dark-skinned man in uniform stepped up to Mandie and reached for her cat. She moved back and said, "No, thank you, I'll carry him."

The man insisted on taking the cat.

Mandie shook her head and repeated, "I'll take him inside. He's afraid of strangers and might scratch you."

Senator Morton turned back and said, "Miss Amanda, that is Juan. He can't hear or speak." He reached to touch the man on his shoulder and shook his head as he motioned with his hands for the man to go ahead. "No," he mouthed to the man.

Juan smiled at Mandie and then went to help the other servants with the luggage.

Mandie walked close to Celia and said under her breath, "That poor man can't hear or talk. How awful!"

"Yes," Celia agreed. "He scared me, insisting on taking Snowball from you."

Mandie bent closer to her friend and said, "I think I'll try to avoid him while we're here. We may have some more misunderstandings."

"Good idea," Celia replied.

The girls were delighted to find that Senator Morton did have a friendly and helpful woman housekeeper. She was waiting just inside the front door for them. They saw Mrs. Taft being escorted toward the staircase by another servant, a younger woman with long, shiny black hair.

"I will show you room," the woman said. She pointed to herself and said, "Name Maria." She was short and plump and middle-aged.

"Thank you," Mandie told Maria as the woman turned to lead the way to the stairs. She noticed she seemed to waddle rather than take definite steps. Mandie and Celia exchanged smiles as they followed the woman up the stairs.

Maria opened the door to a bedroom and stepped aside for the girls to enter. "Put both in same room," she explained. Looking back she added, "Trunk come."

Mandie and Celia both turned and saw two servants bringing their trunks up the steps. They went into the room and showed the men where to set the luggage. As the men left, Maria told Mandie, "Box for cat. There." She motioned toward the far corner.

Mandie rushed across the room and dropped Snowball into the box filled with pure white beach sand. "Thank you," Mandie told the woman.

Maria smiled and stepped inside the room, going toward the trunks. "I unpack," she said, bending to open Mandie's luggage.

Mandie quickly came to her side and pulled a key out of her handbag. She unlocked the trunk while Celia opened hers.

"We can hang up our things," Celia told the woman.

"No, no, I do," Maria insisted as she took a dress from Mandie's trunk, shook out the folds, and went to hang it in a huge wardrobe on the other side of the room.

"Oh well," Mandie said, walking over to the window, which gave them a good view of the town. There were people walking about, many houses nearby, and what looked like business buildings in the distance. She was anxious to explore and wondered when she and Celia could get away from the adults and venture out on their own. This was going to be an interesting city. She may not run across any mystery to be solved here, but she was sure there were lots of things to explore.

When Maria had finished emptying the trunks, she told the girls, "Tea . . . parlor . . . few minutes."

"Tea," Mandie repeated, smiling at Maria. "I could use a cup of tea or something after that long train ride."

"Yes," Celia agreed.

The girls quickly freshened up after Maria left. They combed their hair and straightened their skirts rather than changing clothes. While they were discussing the senator and his house and servants, there was a knock on their door.

"I'll see who it is," Mandie said, crossing the room to open the door. She was surprised to see the tall man named Juan standing outside. "Well?" she asked, moving her shoulders.

Juan smiled and motioned with his hands that they should go downstairs. Then he put one hand up to his mouth like he was drinking from a cup.

Mandie frowned as she nodded her head in the affirmative and said, "Thank you," even though she knew he could not hear her. She started to close the door, but Juan quickly held the door and motioned to go down the stairs.

Celia had come up behind Mandie. "He's telling us he'll show us the way, I believe, Mandie," she said.

"All right. Let's go," Mandie agreed. She looked back and noticed that Snowball had already curled up on the big bed.

Juan led them to the parlor and then left. Senator Morton and Mrs. Taft were already in the room, and another maid, whom they had not seen earlier, brought in the tea tray behind them. The girls sat down near the adults.

"How many servants does one man have?" Mandie said to her friend under her breath.

"Probably a dozen," Celia exaggerated with a short laugh.

After everyone had finished their tea, Mrs. Taft said to the senator, "We have been cramped up in that train so long, I believe I would like to walk about for a little while."

"I was going to suggest that very thing," Senator Morton agreed as he smiled at her.

"That is a very good suggestion, Grandmother," Mandie spoke up.

"Yes," Celia agreed.

"Then let's be on our way," Mrs. Taft said, rising from her chair.

"Just let me run back up to the room and get Snowball. I'm sure he needs some exercise," Mandie said, starting for the door.

"Don't take too long, dear," Mrs. Taft called to her.

Mandie ran up the stairway to the room that she and Celia had been assigned. Just as she started to push the door open, it suddenly opened from the inside, and there stood Juan on the other side.

"What were you doing in our room?" she quickly asked, a bit startled by him.

The man completely ignored her question and seemed in a hurry to get down the hall.

Mandie was upset as she watched him leave, then she remembered that he could not hear. Rushing inside the bedroom, she picked up Snowball, fastened on his red leash, and turned to leave the room. She stopped and looked about, checking to see whether anything had been disturbed. Everything seemed to be as they had left it. She wondered what the man had been doing in their room. It was not likely that Senator Morton would send a male servant up to their room for anything when he had so many women working for him.

Holding Snowball tightly in her arms, Mandie shivered a little and pulled the door closed as she stepped into the hallway. This was a strange situation. She could think of no reason for the man to come into their room. And she hoped she could avoid him. There was something sinister about him. Never in her thirteen years had she met up with such a strange man.

Chapter 2 / The Mystery Continues

Snowball pranced ahead of Mandie, pulling tightly on his leash, as Mandie walked beside Celia down the narrow street. The girls whispered as they watched Mrs. Taft hold on to the senator's arm. "Grandmother is acting like she's old and decrepit, holding on there like she's going to fall," Mandie said, giggling behind her hand.

"She certainly is," Celia agreed, smiling at her friend. "We'd better not get too close behind them or they'll hear what we're saying."

"But we can't get too far behind or Grandmother will look back and tell us to hurry up," Mandie replied. Then, leaning closer to Celia as they walked on, she added, "I didn't get a chance to tell you without them hearing me, but when I went to our room to get Snowball, that man who can't hear or speak was coming out of our room—"

"You don't say!" Celia interrupted, quickly moving a little closer to Mandie. "What was he doing in our room?"

"I don't know. I was wondering the same thing myself," Mandie replied. "When we go back, we'd better look through all our things to see if anything was disturbed."

"Amanda! Celia!" Mrs. Taft called to them as she paused to look back. "That's the old fort up ahead there." She was pointing toward a huge structure down the road.

"Oh, the one the Spaniards built back in sixteen hundred and something!" Mandie excitedly replied as the girls stopped to look ahead.

"I remember reading all about it," Celia added.

"Are we going to see it, Grandmother?" Mandie asked.

"Not right now, but we will while we're here," Mrs. Taft told her. She started back in the direction from which they had come. "I think we should go back and rest a little while now."

"Yes, I know you must all be tired," Senator Morton agreed, also retracing his steps as he held his arm out for Mrs. Taft, which she quickly took.

Mandie and Celia smiled at each other and followed. Snowball tried to get free, but his mistress held tightly to his leash, and he had to go with them.

Mrs. Taft turned her head to glance back at the girls. "Tomorrow we can take the ferry and go over to see the lighthouse, if you girls would like."

Mandie skipped ahead to get closer to her grandmother. "Get a ferry? We have to get a ferry to go see the lighthouse?" she asked.

"Yes, it's on Anastasia Island over that way," Mrs. Taft said, waving her hand to the right.

"It's not far," Senator Morton spoke up as they paused on the street. "You see, our town is surrounded by rivers and bays and such. We are on the very edge of the land going out to sea."

"So we will be able to go out to the beach, like we did at the beach in Charleston when we visited Tommy Patton, then?" Mandie asked, trying to keep Snowball still at the end of his leash.

"Yes, we have a beach," the senator told her. "Our beach is known for its beautiful white sand."

"I remember seeing the white sand as we came down on the train," Mandie said.

"Now let's get on back, girls," Mrs. Taft told them. "We probably have time to rest a little before we change clothes for the evening meal." She started to walk ahead with the senator.

When they got back to Senator Morton's house, the girls went to their room and began inspecting everything for any sign of Juan's having been there.

"Everything looks like it's right where I left it," Mandie remarked after looking over her personal belongings.

"I don't see anything that's been disturbed," Celia agreed.

"I just can't imagine why the man was in our room," Mandie said, walking around. "Maybe I came in as soon as he had stepped inside, and he hadn't had time to do whatever he had come in here for."

Celia agreed as she flopped on the ivory crocheted counterpane on the big bed, where Snowball had curled up. "You're probably right," she said.

Mandie walked over to the huge mahogany

wardrobe and opened the door. "Now, what am I going to wear down to supper tonight?" she said to herself. She reached inside to look through her dresses that Maria had hung there. Frowning, she added, "Now, that's strange. Half of my clothes are hung one way and the other half the other way."

Celia quickly came up behind her and asked, "What do you mean, Mandie?" She looked over Mandie's shoulder at the contents of the wardrobe.

"Maria hung up all our clothes, remember? Now, why would she hang them two different ways?" Mandie asked, puzzled.

"Oh, Mandie, so are mine!" Celia exclaimed. "Mine are split up that way, too." She reached to examine her dresses.

Maria had hung all of Mandie's clothes on the left side of the wardrobe and Celia's on the right.

"Well, I'm going to turn mine all the same way, and I am going to ask Maria about this when I get a chance," Mandie said, quickly taking down each dress and rehanging it in the right direction.

Celia watched as Mandie rearranged her clothes and then said, "Now let me do mine. It makes me feel like I'm cross-eyed or something to look at dresses hanging two different ways."

Mandie stepped back while Celia rearranged hers.

"And now we'd better decide what we are going to put on," Mandie told her.

Celia took down a pale green voile dress and moved out of Mandie's way as she said, "I think I'll wear this one."

"And I'll wear my white one with the red embroidery," Mandie quickly decided, removing a frilly white dress with red rosebuds embroidered all over it.

The girls quickly took off their travel clothes, freshened up in the bathroom, and put on their fresh dresses.

Mandie went to look at her dress in the full-length mirror that was on a stand in the corner. She straightened her long, full skirt and tied the red sash around her waist, while Celia used the mirror on the huge bureau. Mandie glanced out the open window and said, "We have a view of the park up the street from here, and I do believe I see Juan walking through it. Come look."

Celia hurried to her side and said, "Yes, that does look like Juan. I suppose Senator Morton has sent him on an errand." She turned back to the mirror to brush her long auburn curls.

"Probably," Mandie agreed, fluffing out the huge bow on the back of her dress where she had tied the sash.

As Celia pulled back her hair with a ribbon to match her green dress, she said, "I wonder what time we are supposed to go downstairs? I don't remember anyone telling us, do you?"

"I don't think so, but I suppose someone will come to let us know," Mandie replied, twirling around in front of the long mirror. She stopped and looked at her friend. "I wish some of our friends could have come with us. This is going to be a poky, uninteresting two weeks, I'm afraid." She went to sit in a chair nearby. "And I just don't know why Joe Woodard had to go off to a college so far away as New Orleans when there are lots of other colleges much nearer home."

"Oh, Mandie," Celia said with a loud sigh as

she sat down in another chair, carefully spreading out her skirts as she did so. "You know why. That's the college that accepted him even though he didn't have all the subjects required for admission."

"I know," Mandie said, blowing out her breath. "And he has to work real hard to catch up for the entrance into the regular college level in the fall. It all sounds so complicated. I'm glad our school will have us prepared for college when we finish there." She paused and looked at her friend. "I wonder where Tommy Patton and Robert are planning to go to college?"

"Since they aren't both going to finish Mr. Chadwick's school for boys for two more years, they have time to decide," Celia replied, smiling.

Mandie smiled back. "I know exactly what you're thinking," she teased. "You are hoping you and Robert Rogers will go to the same college."

Celia fluttered her eyelids, looked away across the room, and said, "Well, it would be nice to have someone at college that I already know."

"And it would be nice if your mother agrees to whatever you're planning," Mandie added.

"That goes for you, too. Don't forget, your mother might just send you off to New York or somewhere else way off for college," Celia reminded her.

"But don't forget, I have two more years at school to talk her out of anything I don't want to do," Mandie replied with a big grin. "Besides, Uncle John is always on my side."

"I know," Celia agreed. "Aren't you glad he married your mother?"

Mandie's smile faded as she replied, "Since I

lost my father, I'm glad I have Uncle John, because he's my father's brother."

"I envy you. I don't have a father or an uncle," Celia said sadly.

"But you do have Aunt Rebecca," Mandie reminded her, "and I don't even have an aunt." She rose to walk back over to the window and look out.

At that moment someone knocked on their door, and Celia went to open it. Mandie turned to see who it was. The maid who had taken Mrs. Taft to her room when they arrived was standing there.

"Downstairs," the girl was saying. "Now."

"Oh yes, thank you," Celia replied.

"We'll be right down," Mandie added. She walked across the room as Celia closed the door.

Both girls glanced in the mirror one final time and then went down to the parlor. They left Snowball asleep on the bed.

Mrs. Taft and Senator Morton were seated near a French door that opened out to a patio. They stopped talking and looked up when the girls entered the room.

"The cat, Amanda, did you leave the cat in your room and close the door?" Mrs. Taft asked.

The girls sat down on a small settee near the adults.

"Yes, ma'am," Mandie replied. "He was asleep on the bed, and he has a sandbox in our room, so he'll be all right till it's time to feed him."

"Are you sure he doesn't know how to open the door?" Senator Morton joked with a big grin.

Mandie looked at him thoughtfully and said, "I'm not sure. Snowball has done some intelligent things, like untying knots in ropes and leaving a room by way of the chimney when the door was closed. But I can't remember him ever opening a door, unless it was partly open, of course, and I made sure our door was closed." She laughed.

"Yes, I remember some incidences with him on the ship when we all went to Europe. I'd say he is a very educated cat," the senator said, still grinning.

"Educated," Mandie repeated and looked at her grandmother. "What will I do with him when I go away to college? Will they allow me to bring Snowball with me? I can't go way off to school somewhere and leave Snowball home all that time."

"Amanda, I don't believe they would allow a cat to live at any college, so don't plan on it," Mrs. Taft replied.

Mandie worried for a moment and then said, "Grandmother, I know what we can do. You could just buy a college somewhere . . . like you bought the school where Celia and I go . . . and then we could make our own rules."

"Amanda, buying a girls' school and buying a college are two quite different transactions," Mrs. Taft told her. "Besides, you won't be going off to college for another two years. By that time you will have to get used to the fact that you will not be able to take that cat everywhere you go."

"Oh," Mandie muttered to herself.

"In the meantime, we'll take Snowball sight-seeing with us tomorrow," Senator Morton told her.

"Thank you, Senator," Mandie said. "And thank you for allowing me to bring Snowball to your house."

"He's just as welcome as you are, dear, anytime. I had a dog when I was your age, and I wouldn't go anywhere my dog was not welcome. I understand," the senator said with a smile. "And Zeke lived to be almost fifteen years old, so he got in a lot of traveling in his lifetime."

"I know it must have been sad when Zeke died," Mandie said. "Snowball is already over two years old. His birthday was January fifteenth. You see, after my father died, I brought Snowball with me when I went to stay with Uncle John."

"That's not old at all. He has many more years ahead of him," Senator Morton said. He suddenly looked beyond Mandie, who had her back to the door, and said, "Thank you, Juan." He then rose and said, "I believe the food is on the table."

Mandie quickly turned to look at the door. Juan was standing there, making motions that evidently meant it was time to go eat. She thought he must not have gone far when she saw him crossing the park, and he must get around quickly. He seemed to turn up everywhere.

Mandie and Celia followed the adults to the dining room, where they both looked excitedly around the huge room. There were large French doors at both ends with lots of floor-length windows in between. The floor was made of polished stone and was covered down the middle with a carpet of many brilliant colors, on which the long table stood. Plants grew in pots inside the windows. A great stone fireplace took up almost one whole wall, guarded by suits of armor at either end. Above it, swords and paintings of old ancestors in antique frames covered the wall. The table had approximately twenty-six chairs around it, which Mandie quickly tried to count. Several ornate silver candelabras stood along the middle of the table. Crystal chandeliers hung from the high ceiling at each end of the room.

Senator Morton led them to the table, and Mandie was glad to see they were all placed at one end. She imagined trying to talk from one end to the other! Also, she tried to imagine what it was like for Senator Morton to eat alone at the huge table, but then she thought he probably had another small dining room somewhere in the big house where he ate his meals when he didn't have guests.

As they sat down, Mandie noticed several servants hovering around the sideboards that held the food along one wall. Senator Morton seemed to have plenty of everything—house, servants, food, and all.

Mandie watched as the servants served the food, but she didn't see Juan among them. Evidently he had only come to let the senator know that the meal was ready and had then gone elsewhere. Mandie suddenly wondered where the man was. Had he gone back to their room? He knew they were in the dining room and would be there for a while. She leaned close to speak to Celia as she watched the senator and her grandmother occupied with their own conversation at the table.

"Where did Juan go?" she whispered.

Celia quickly looked around the room. "I don't see him," she whispered back.

"He's not in this room," Mandie spoke softly again.

"No, he isn't," Celia agreed.

During the entire meal, Mandie was wishing the time away so she could go upstairs and check their room. She tried and tried to think of some excuse to leave the table for a few minutes, but she couldn't come up with any that she thought would meet with her grandmother's approval.

Mrs. Taft and Senator Morton mostly kept up their own conversation, but now and then they would say something to the girls. Mandie only gave short answers to anything they said to her. She didn't want to be drawn into a conversation with them because she wanted to watch the room in case Juan returned.

Finally it was time for dessert. Mandie was enjoying the seven-layer chocolate cake with creamy icing when she thought she saw a flash of white near the door to the hallway. Then she almost choked when Snowball suddenly appeared under her chair and began rubbing around her legs. Someone had let him out of their room.

"Snowball!" she exclaimed, pushing back her chair to reach down and pick him up. She stood up, quickly looked at her grandmother and the senator, and said, "I'm sorry. I'll take him back upstairs." She started toward the door.

Both Mrs. Taft and Senator Morton looked at her and the cat in surprise.

"Wait," the senator said. "He needs to be fed anyway, so I'll get someone to take him out to the kitchen." He started to push back his chair.

But Mandie was determined to check out their room immediately. "I'll be right back," she called to her grandmother as she rushed out of the room.

Keeping an eye out for Juan, Mandie hurried down the hallway to the stairs. She took the steps two at a time, almost tripping on her long skirts until she reached down and pulled them up with one hand. She didn't see a single servant until she got to the hallway where their room was. Then suddenly a man came walking toward her, a man whom she had not seen before. He was tall and dark, with a thin mustache and curly black hair. She was not exactly sure where he had come from. There was a short cross hall before their room, and he could have been in any of the rooms around that corner.

When the man saw her, he turned and went the other direction. She hurried on to her room. The door was shut tightly, and she knew immediately that someone had to have let Snowball out.

"Be quiet, Snowball," she whispered to the cat as he clung to her shoulder. She slowly opened the door to her room.

Quietly crossing the room, she looked around behind the furniture and in the bathroom. No one was there. She couldn't see that anything had been disturbed.

"But someone was definitely in here," she whispered to her cat. "How I wish you could talk." She set him down and added, "I've got to go back. Now, if anyone else comes in here, you just hiss and scratch them for all you're worth, you hear?"

"Meow," Snowball agreed as he jumped up on the bed and began walking in circles before he settled down and curled up.

"And don't get too comfortable, either," Mandie cautioned him. "I will be back soon to get you for your supper."

Still looking around the room, she went back to the door, opened it, stepped into the hallway, and closed the door firmly. She checked it to be sure it wouldn't come open.

As she hurried back down to the dining room, she wondered who the man was she had seen on the upper floor. Senator Morton seemed to have different servants at every turn she made. He had so many servants that she wondered how he kept up with all of them, especially since he spent a great deal of time in Washington. Because he was away a lot, he would have to have people working for him whom he could trust, but somehow she just didn't trust Juan. She wondered where he was.

Chapter 3 / The Lighthouse Visit

Everyone retired to their rooms early that night. Mandie and Celia got ready for bed, but they were too excited to go to sleep. They walked over to an open window and knelt down to lean on the windowsill and gaze out into the darkness. Many lights were still visible in other houses.

"I wish we didn't have to waste time sleeping. I want to see everything," Mandie fussed, pushing back her long blond hair.

"But sleeping is not wasting time, Mandie," Celia reminded her. "If we didn't sleep, we would soon run out of the strength to go on. I'm sure we'd feel absolutely awful."

"Back home, when I mentioned we were coming to St. Augustine, so many people told me to see this or do that. There must be lots to do here in this town," Mandie said.

"I've heard that, too," Celia agreed. "My mother has visited here before, and she was saying—"

Mandie quickly leaned her head out the window as she interrupted, "Celia, isn't that Juan walking up the street over there? That way, toward the park." She pointed.

Celia pushed forward to see. "It looks like him."

"I wonder where he's going this time of night?" Mandie said, watching the figure move quickly up the street and into the distance.

"Mandie, there are lots of places he could be going," Celia replied. "He lives in this town, you know."

"But he's headed for the same park where we saw him go before," Mandie said, squinting to see into the darkness that now blocked Juan from her view.

Celia moved back inside the window and said, "We'll have to give up on him tonight. He's gone."

Mandie turned back into the room on her knees. "Oh well, we have lots of other things to talk about," she said. "I have even heard that St. Augustine has ghosts. Can you imagine, ghosts?"

"Ghosts?" Celia questioned. "Do you believe in such things?"

"Just that they're some kind of mystery someone is trying to make," Mandie replied with a big smile. "I'm sure I could solve the whole thing if we happened on to one of these so-called ghosts."

"But suppose there really is such a thing as a ghost?" Celia asked. She shivered as she added, "I sure hope we don't run into one."

Mandie laughed and said, "I'll take care of it if we do. It might be fun to solve a mystery about a ghost, because I'm sure there aren't any real ghosts."

Mandie was so certain there was no such thing

as a ghost that she had no problem falling asleep later. But her certainty was shaken the next morning in their conversation at breakfast. Mrs. Taft and Senator Morton were discussing several points of interest they thought the girls might like to visit.

"I would say top preference should be given to the old fort," Mrs. Taft said, looking around the table. "A tour of it would be both educational and interesting."

"Yes, ma'am, you are so right," Senator Morton agreed, setting down his coffee cup. Looking at Mandie and Celia, he asked, "Would you young ladies like to visit some of our ghost-occupied places?"

"Ghosts? Real ghosts?" Celia asked, laying down her fork.

"Yes, Miss Celia, what some people declare are ghosts," Senator Morton replied.

Mandie was speechless with surprise for a moment. Then she asked, "Grown-up people believe in ghosts?"

"There are some adults who do, Miss Amanda," the senator told her.

Mrs. Taft spoke from across the table. "Amanda, there's nothing unusual about that. There have always been some people who believe in such things," she said. "I never have, but I have known others who absolutely have sworn they have seen ghosts."

Mandie looked back at the senator and asked, "And you know people here in St. Augustine who actually believe in ghosts, you say?"

"Oh yes, in fact, I'll introduce you and Miss Celia to some of these folks," Senator Morton promised.

Mandie thought about the possibility of meeting

someone who actually believed in ghosts. She didn't believe anyone could actually confirm that they had seen a ghost because in her opinion there were no such things as ghosts. She could easily solve such a mystery, just as she had told Celia.

"Amanda, Celia, if we're going to spend time out at the lighthouse, we should hurry now and get finished with our breakfast," Mrs. Taft reminded the girls.

"Oh yes, ma'am," Mandie replied quickly, then drank her coffee.

"I am already finished," Celia announced as she laid her knife and fork across her empty plate.

"So am I," Mandie added, setting down her empty cup.

"Then I'll see about our basket of food that the cook is preparing for us to take along," Senator Morton said, rising from the table.

"We'll get our hats and wait for you in the parlor, then," Mrs. Taft told him as she, too, stood up.

"I'll get Snowball," Mandie said, rising and following the senator toward the kitchen, where her cat had been given his breakfast while they ate.

As they walked down the hall toward the kitchen door, Mandie asked the senator, "Do you really know people who believe in ghosts, Senator Morton?"

The senator stopped to look down at her and said, "I certainly do, and I have an idea you are anxious to meet them." He smiled at her.

"Yes, sir, I am," Mandie agreed. "I just never knew anyone who believed in ghosts, and I have lots of questions to ask these people. Do you think I could question them?"

"Why, you certainly can, Miss Amanda," he replied as he pushed open the door to the kitchen. "In fact, that kind of people always like to talk about what they've seen and heard."

"I'm glad it's all right," Mandie said, following him into the kitchen, where Snowball came running to her. "Let's go, Snowball," she said, picking up the white cat. She glanced at Senator Morton, who had gone down to the other end of the long room and was talking to the cook.

Mandie carried Snowball and hurried upstairs to her room to get his leash and her hat. Celia was ready and waiting.

"I suppose we have to be nice to these people who believe in ghosts. When we meet them, we better not stare," Celia said, following Mandie across the room.

Mandie reached for Snowball's leash on the bureau and turned to look at her friend. "And not stare?" she asked. "Now, why would we stare at people like that?" She stooped to fasten Snowball's leash.

"Well, I figure they must be strange people to believe in such things," Celia explained.

Mandie quickly stood up, rushed over to the wardrobe, and got her straw hat. "They probably are a little odd," she agreed as she stood in front of the mirror to put on her hat. "But we can still be polite to them. Besides, I want to ask them lots of questions, so I know I'll have to be nice to them if I want any answers. Come on. Let's go." She quickly picked up Snowball and headed for the door. Celia followed.

Even though it was only a short distance to the dock to get the ferry that traveled back and forth to Anastasia Island, Senator Morton had Juan waiting with his carriage to drive them there.

The girls sat in the backseat, and while the senator and Mrs. Taft were busy talking, Mandie whispered to her friend, "I would think it's dangerous for Juan to drive if he can't hear."

"But he can see," Celia whispered back.

Mandie held on to Snowball in her lap as they turned a corner. "He can't see forward, backward, and to both sides at one time—like your ears can hear in every direction."

"Well," Celia replied thoughtfully, "I suppose you are right. But maybe other drivers in this town know he can't hear and watch out for him and stay out of his way."

"I hope so," Mandie said. "He is a strange person. I've been wondering about his friends. How can he communicate with them? He can't carry on a conversation."

"The poor man may not have many friends," Celia said.

"I sure wish he could talk. I'd like to ask him why he was in our room," Mandie said. She bent closer to her friend and added, "Maybe we can follow him sometime, when we see him leave Senator Morton's house."

"Are you serious?" Celia asked in surprise.

"I don't trust him." Then she quickly added, "You know, he may have a family here in town somewhere. He may not actually live at the senator's house. What do you think?"

"Yes, that could be so," Celia agreed.

"Maybe we can find out somehow or other," Mandie said. Straightening up in her seat, she saw the dock coming into view. "This must be the place where we get the ferryboat. See the water and all the little boats tied up there."

Mrs. Taft turned from her seat to look back at the girls. "Amanda, please be careful with that cat," she said. "We would never find him if he got away from you here."

"Yes, ma'am," Mandie replied, squeezing Snowball tightly in her arms as the carriage rolled to a stop. "Snowball, you heard Grandmother. You'd better behave now," she added, looking down into the white cat's blue eyes.

Snowball meowed in response and reached a paw up to touch her face.

The cat did behave well on the ferry. But once they landed and stepped ashore, he decided he wanted to run away, forcing Mandie to carry him. Out of the corner of her eye, she noticed Juan watching her as he carried the picnic basket, and she hurried to walk near the senator. She wished one of the other servants had come with them instead of Juan.

"Mandie, look how big the lighthouse is!" Celia exclaimed as they neared the structure.

Mandie gazed up and asked, "Do you suppose we can go all the way to the top of it?"

Senator Morton, walking ahead with Mrs. Taft, heard the question and turned to reply, "Of course you young ladies may go all the way to the top if you wish, but my legs are not as young as they used to be, so I'll stay on the ground."

"So will I," Mrs. Taft added as she and the senator paused in front of the girls. "However, Amanda, you and Celia may walk up to the observation tower, provided you don't let that cat get loose. That would cause a lot of trouble."

"I'll hold on to him, Grandmother," Mandie promised.

Mrs. Taft and Senator Morton sat down on a bench near the entrance to the lighthouse to wait for the girls. Mandie and Celia went inside and began the long climb to the top. Mandie happened to glance back from the first landing and saw Juan also coming up the steps.

"Don't look back," Mandie whispered to Celia as they continued on their way, "but Juan is behind us."

"Oh no!" Celia whispered back without turning.

At that moment, Mandie tripped on her long skirts, and Snowball managed to get free. He raced up the stairs ahead of them and disappeared around a corner. Mandie quickly pulled up her skirts and sprinted after him.

"The leash came unhooked," she told Celia as her friend ran with her up the steps. She held up the red leash, which she had wrapped around her wrist to prevent Snowball from escaping. "Snowball! Come back here!" she called up the stairs.

Other people going up the stairs moved aside as the girls raced past them. Mandie kept watching for the cat and was surprised to see Juan quickly pass them, evidently in pursuit of the cat.

Carefully inspecting each turn in the stairs, Mandie kept calling, "Snowball, come back here!"

Celia, gasping for breath as she stayed right behind Mandie, said, "I just hope he doesn't fall out a window!"

"Oh no!" Mandie cried, glancing back at her friend and hurrying faster.

Finally the girls reached the top and came out onto the observation deck. Mandie heard Snowball squealing before she saw him. Juan was stooping near the rail and was holding Snowball by his collar as the cat tried to get loose. He was trying his best to bite and scratch Juan, who somehow managed to avoid the fight.

Mandie rushed to fasten the leash to Snowball's collar. Juan immediately stood up and hurried back down the stairs without looking directly at Mandie.

"Thank you, Juan," Mandie called to him, even though she knew he could not hear her. After securely hooking the leash, Mandie picked up her cat. "Snowball, just wait until Grandmother hears about you running off like that. If you don't start behaving better, one day she's going to stop letting you go places with us."

Snowball purred.

"Look, Mandie!" Celia exclaimed from the railing. "You can see forever from here!" She waved her hand around in the air.

Mandie joined her at the rail and looked out over the water, which disappeared into the distance. The bouncing waves glowed in the bright sunshine, ushering a strong salt-laden breeze up the shore. The girls had to hold their hats with one hand and their long, full skirts with the other. Since Mandie had Snowball on her shoulder, she bent her arm around him and tried to hold her hat with that hand. Finally she leaned against the rail to keep her skirts from billowing out.

"How beautiful!" Mandie exclaimed as she took a deep breath of the fresh, salty air. Looking at Celia, she said, "I wonder why Juan didn't stay up here to look at the scenery after he made the long climb up."

"Yes, he was already going up when Snowball

escaped, so he didn't come up for just that," Celia commented as she continued to turn and survey the view from the lighthouse. "But he sure left in a hurry when you took Snowball from him."

"Let's walk around to the other side and see what we can see from there," Mandie said, grasping Snowball firmly in her arms as she slowly moved around the huge tower.

Celia followed, holding tightly to her hat and skirts as the wind continued to blow. "Don't go too fast, Mandie," she said. "It's hard to move around in this wind."

"Now we can see back the way we came," Mandie remarked as she stopped to gaze at the people who were walking in the direction of the ferry they had come on.

Celia came to her side and looked down. "I can't see your grandmother and the senator down there. But they sat so close to the lighthouse, we probably can't see that part of the grounds from up here."

"Yes," Mandie agreed as she peered off into the departing crowd. Suddenly she reached to touch Celia's arm. "Celia! Look! That woman down there in the black dress and hat!" she exclaimed. "That looks like the strange woman who followed us around when we went to Europe! Remember?" She bent forward to stare below.

"Where?" Celia asked and looked in the direction Mandie was pointing. "I can't tell from up here. She's so far away, but I see the woman you're talking about."

"I'm pretty sure it's her! Come on, let's see if we can catch up with her!" Mandie exclaimed, quickly turning to rush toward the steps.

Celia followed as Mandie practically flew down

to the ground level. "She was too far away. She'll be gone," she said as she gasped for breath and raced outside after Mandie.

"Come on!" Mandie called back as she squeezed Snowball tightly and continued running in the direction the crowd had gone. They were completely out of sight now.

Finally Mandie gave up and dropped onto a bench along the way. She was so out of breath that she couldn't speak for a few minutes. Celia sat by her, also trying to catch her breath. Snowball meowed loudly.

"Oh, shucks!" Mandie finally managed to say. "She's gone!"

"Right," Celia agreed, straightening her long skirts and her hat.

"I'm almost certain it was that woman," Mandie said, pushing her straw hat back in place. "I wonder what she was doing here."

"Mandie, if it was that woman, she was probably just visiting like we are," Celia replied, still breathing hard.

"Well, it sure is odd that we should run into her all the way down here in Florida," Mandie remarked.

"And, Mandie, we don't know for certain that it was that woman," Celia reminded her. "It could have been someone who just looked like her."

Mandie smiled and said, "There is no one who could even resemble her. Remember how she used to turn up everywhere we went in Europe, and how she used to meddle in our business about Jonathan? She is one of a kind, I can assure you."

"Oh, I remember that, all right," Celia agreed.

"She thought we weren't very ladylike sometimes." She smiled.

"Well, I suppose we should go back to the lighthouse," Mandie said, rising and shaking out her skirts.

"Yes, before your grandmother misses us," Celia agreed. She got up and once more straightened her hat.

As the girls walked back the way they had come, Mandie was surprised to see Juan coming toward them. She whispered to Celia, "Look, there's Juan. I wonder where he's going this time?"

"I don't know," Celia whispered back as the man, seeing them, suddenly stepped to one side of the pathway.

Mandie led the way, knowing she would have to pass Juan and feeling a little afraid of him. Why was he following them around, and what was he doing standing right in the middle of the way?

"Ignore him," Mandie whispered to Celia as they walked on.

Both girls looked the other way when they passed Juan. They hurried on down the lane toward the lighthouse and rushed around to the side where they had left Mrs. Taft and Senator Morton. The adults were still sitting on the bench.

"Amanda, where were you and Celia going in such a big hurry?" Mrs. Taft asked as the two young people came up.

"I sent Juan after y'all to see if something was wrong," the senator added.

"You did?" Mandie asked with a sigh of relief. "Grandmother, do you remember that strange woman on the ship who followed us all over Europe last summer? Well, I believe she was here. We were trying to catch up with her, but she was too far ahead with the crowd going back to the ferry."

"Amanda, are you sure?" Mrs. Taft asked.

"I'm pretty sure, Grandmother," Mandie replied.

"It did look like her," Celia added.

"You young ladies are speaking of Miss Lucretia Wham, I take it?" Senator Morton asked.

"Yes, sir, that's the strange woman's name," Mandie agreed.

"This could be very interesting, having her show up here in St. Augustine," the senator said thoughtfully.

"But the girls are not positive it was Miss Wham," Mrs. Taft reminded him.

Mandie smiled at her grandmother's precise way of deciding matters. "But I am half positive, I'd say," Mandie told her.

"If that was Miss Wham, we will find out sooner or later," Senator Morton remarked.

Mandie wondered what he meant by that remark. How would he find out whether it was the strange woman from the ship? And what was the woman doing in St. Augustine?

Mandie and Celia discussed the woman the rest of the day. And then at one point of recalling the events of the day, Mandie suddenly wondered how the senator had communicated with Juan, who couldn't hear, and asked him to follow her and Celia. There were too many unanswered questions, and she meant to find the answers.

Chapter 4 / The Old Fort

The next day, which was Wednesday, May 28, was another day full of mystery and unanswered questions. Mandie and Celia went with Mrs. Taft and Senator Morton to visit the old fort that the Spanish had begun building in 1672 and finished in 1695, while Spain owned Florida. Juan accompanied them this time, too, with another picnic basket full of food.

"What a huge building!" Mandie exclaimed as she held on to Snowball and stopped to look ahead.

"Yes, and it's the oldest masonry fort in the United States," Senator Morton added as the others paused in front of it.

"Is it still a fort? I see men in uniforms walking around over there." Mandie pointed toward one side.

"Yes, it's still a fort, but we will be allowed to go inside," the senator replied. He stepped ahead and spoke with one of the men, then motioned for the others to follow him.

"Amanda, please hold on to that cat while we're inside. It gets rather dark in places, and he could get lost forever," Mrs. Taft told Mandie as they joined the senator.

"Yes, ma'am," Mandie replied, looping the end of Snowball's red leash around her wrist and checking the hook to the collar. "He'll be all right, Grandmother."

"I'll help you carry him," Celia offered as they followed the adults into the fort.

The light was dim, but Mandie could see men here and there, going about their business, whatever it was. Senator Morton spoke to several people as they continued through the building, and he turned to recite historical facts about the fort now and then. Everything looked old and dark with lots of nooks and crannies, and eventually they ended up in the cellar.

"This is really scary down here," Celia remarked, moving closer to Mandie as everyone stopped in the center of a large room.

Mandie grinned at her friend and said, "Yes, awfully mysterious." She glanced back the way they had come and realized Juan was no longer with them. "Where's Juan?" she added in a whisper to her friend.

Celia looked around and shrugged.

"When the British owned Florida during the Revolutionary War, they used it for prisoners after they captured Charleston, South Carolina," Senator Morton was saying as the girls turned back to listen. "In fact, three signers of the Declaration of Independence were imprisoned here."

Mandie was only half listening as she kept glancing around. Where did Juan go? And what was he doing? She was anxious to keep moving on through the place so she could eventually find the man.

Senator Morton stepped into one of the cells as he talked, and Mrs. Taft followed him.

Mandie instantly pulled Celia's hand and raced around the corner of a wall to look for Juan. Celia hurried behind her.

"Mandie, where are you going? We'll get lost in this spooky place," Celia complained.

"No, we won't. I'm looking for Juan," Mandie whispered, holding tightly to Snowball, who was protesting the fast movement.

Mandie quickly looked around every corner in the darkness and was about to return to the adults when she suddenly spotted Juan and another man standing in one of the small rooms. The man was talking rapidly in a low voice, and she could not hear what he was saying. But Juan was looking directly at the man as though he could hear every word.

"Sh-h-h!" Mandie whispered as she put out a hand to stop her friend and pointed ahead. "Look!"

Celia gasped and moved closer to Mandie as she, too, saw the men.

Suddenly, Juan looked into the corridor and saw the girls standing there. He quickly motioned to the other man, who immediately walked off in another direction.

Mandie, a little frightened at being caught, began talking to Snowball as she walked back the way they had come. "Now, Snowball, don't you run off again, you hear?" She squeezed him in her arms. The cat purred loudly.

Celia hurried alongside Mandie and kept glancing back.

"Are we being followed?" Mandie asked as she snuggled Snowball on her shoulder.

"No, he's gone," Celia replied.

As usual, Mandie was more interested in a mystery than in sight-seeing. She spent the rest of the day watching Juan, who joined them as Senator Morton continued leading them through the fort. When they eventually went up on the gun deck, her attention returned.

Rushing over to one side, she exclaimed, "Look, Celia, there's the lighthouse!"

"I can see people down there by the water," Celia added, leaning forward.

Mandie turned to look back at the adults and realized Juan had disappeared again. She sighed as she wondered where he had gone this time.

Senator Morton looked at the girls and said, "In case you young ladies are hungry, I've sent Juan to get the food from the carriage. We will go down by the water and find a place to spread our meal."

Mandie smiled at him and was glad he had solved the disappearance of Juan. "Yes, sir, I'm starving, and so is Snowball," she replied, holding tightly to the white cat and following the adults as they descended the steps.

"So am I," Celia added, hurrying alongside Mandie.

"That other man who was with Juan, I wonder where he went? Keep a watch out for him," Mandie whispered to her friend.

"Mandie, it was so dark in there, I don't think I could recognize him if I saw him," Celia replied.

"Well, anyway, we can observe whether Juan meets up with anyone else around here," Mandie told her.

By the time everyone had walked down to the water, Juan had selected a spot and was spreading out quilts to sit on and a tablecloth for the food. Mrs. Taft and Senator Morton sat on a low wall nearby while the girls got comfortable on the quilts. Mandie looped Snowball's leash around an old rock post near her and breathed a sigh of relief.

"At least we got through that place without Snowball running off," she told Celia.

"Yes, but we aren't finished here yet," Celia agreed.

Juan kept watching the girls as he served the food. Mandie felt uncomfortable with his gaze and ignored it as she talked to Celia of other things.

"I forgot to watch for that strange woman today," Mandie said, suddenly sitting up straight and looking around. "You didn't see her anywhere, did you?"

Celia laughed and said, "Of course not, Mandie. I would have let you know if I had. You know, we aren't even positive that was Miss Wham we saw out at the lighthouse."

"I believe it was," Mandie replied, pushing back a stray strand of hair as the breeze from the water drifted past them. "You know, I wish Jonathan was here. He was involved in that mystery with the woman."

"Mandie!" Celia exclaimed as she accepted a plate of food from Juan and thanked him. "You've been wishing away the time until you can see Joe, and now here you are wishing you could see Jonathan. You are one fickle young lady.'' She laughed teasingly.

Mandie grinned and replied, "Maybe I am, but I have lots of friends and I like them all.'' Juan handed her a plate of food. She looked up at him, smiled, and said, "Thank you.''

To her amazement, Juan smiled back. Did he hear what she said? Well, no, he was deaf, but he could see her smile. That was it. He saw her smile and returned it. She quickly looked down at her food and began eating.

Senator Morton and Mrs. Taft carried on their own conversation. From where Mandie was sitting, she could not hear anything they were saying. But from the expressions on their faces, it seemed to be a serious discussion. Juan sat alone with his food.

"I'll be glad when I can go back home,'' Mandie remarked. "If Joe has not come home by then, maybe he will have written me a letter.''

"But Joe is so busy studying to catch up, he may not have time to write,'' Celia told her as she ate a bite of the potato on her plate.

"I know,'' Mandie agreed. Then lowering her voice, she leaned closer to her friend and said, "At least while we're here with Juan, we know he isn't in our room.''

Celia gasped and looked at the man, who was staring straight at Mandie. "Let's talk about school, Mandie,'' she said. "I'll be glad to go back in the fall so I can see Robert.''

"Robert,'' Mandie repeated with a big grin. "I have an idea you like that fellow. And I know he likes you a whole lot.''

Celia blushed as she replied, "Mandie! How do

you know that?" She stopped eating to look at Mandie.

"Oh, anyone could tell that if they were around you and him long enough," Mandie said with a big grin, swallowing a bite of her food.

Snowball suddenly decided he didn't want to stay tied up. He began meowing and trying to pull loose from the post.

"All right, Snowball, you're hungry. Sorry, but I forgot to give you anything," Mandie told him. She started to take a bite of food from her plate when Juan suddenly handed her a small plate of food for the cat. She looked up at him and smiled again, saying, "Thank you." She took the plate and placed it where Snowball could reach it.

Watching from under lowered eyelids, Mandie saw Juan return to his spot on a rock nearby to finish his food. She felt like she was continuously saying thank-you to the man. Even though he couldn't hear, he always seemed to understand.

After everyone had eaten, Senator Morton led them around the area, and they investigated various old buildings along the way. But finally it was time to return to his house because Mrs. Taft was tired and wanted to rest.

Mandie was tired of being around Juan and wanted to get away from him. Snowball seemed tired, too, so she picked him up as they returned to the carriage.

"It's not time for supper yet, so what are we going to do in the meantime?" Celia asked as they followed the adults to the vehicle.

"When we get back to Senator Morton's, maybe we can stay outside and walk around a little," Mandie suggested.

"All right, provided we don't get lost," Celia agreed.

"This town is so small. How could we get lost?" Mandie asked.

"It's bigger than you think, Mandie," Celia replied.

"All right, we'll just walk all the way around the town and see how big it really is," Mandie said as they stopped by the carriage. Senator Morton helped Mrs. Taft step up into it and followed her inside. Then Juan, who was standing by, walked over to the girls and made a motion that he would assist them into the carriage.

Mandie quickly pulled away from him and rushed inside. Celia was right behind her. As they sat down on the seat, Mandie whispered, "I'm glad that's over with." She held Snowball in her lap.

"Yes," Celia agreed.

When Juan pulled the carriage up in front of Senator Morton's house, he stood back and watched the girls. He did not offer to help them from the carriage. Mandie was anxious to get away from him and hurried into the house right behind the adults.

Mrs. Taft turned to speak to the girls. "We will rest a little, Amanda, and be refreshed for the evening meal," she said.

"Grandmother, would it be all right if Celia and I walk around outside while you rest?" Mandie asked, setting Snowball down at the end of his leash.

Mrs. Taft looked up at Senator Morton without replying, and he said, "I will ask one of the maids to go with them if you like."

"But, Senator Morton, we don't need anyone to

go with us," Mandie protested. "Celia and I walk around all the time without adults escorting us."

"Amanda, this is a strange town to you, and I won't have you going off by yourselves and getting lost or into some kind of predicament," Mrs. Taft quickly told her. "Senator Morton has graciously offered the services of a maid, and if y'all want to go on a walk, then you must allow the maid to accompany you."

"Yes, ma'am," Mandie replied, and then looking up at the senator, she asked, "Do you think we could have Maria go with us, then?"

"Maria?" the senator questioned. "Well, normally that's not her position, but I'll ask her to walk with y'all."

Mandie smiled and said, "Thank you, Senator Morton."

"All right, I'm going up to my room. I want you girls to be on your best ladylike behavior," Mrs. Taft said, walking toward the staircase.

"Yes, ma'am," both girls chorused.

"And I'll get Maria," the senator said, going down the hallway. But when he returned to the parlor, he had the younger maid with the long, shiny black hair with him. "Maria is not here, but Lolly will go with you young ladies. She will walk with you wherever you wish to go, but I have told her to be sure you are all back in time for supper."

The girls thanked the senator, and he left the room as Lolly stood waiting.

Mandie looked at Lolly and said, "We would just like to walk around to see how big this town really is."

"I see," Lolly agreed, going toward the front door. "Then we go."

As they stepped outside, they met Juan, who was coming toward the house. Mandie noticed that Lolly seemed to be all smiles for the man, and he smiled back at her.

"Back soon," Lolly said to Juan as she passed him.

He smiled back again.

Mandie looked at Celia as they followed the girl. Catching up with her, Mandie said, "But Juan can't speak or hear, and you spoke to him."

The girl seemed to be completely flustered as she looked at Mandie. "Juan cannot speak or hear, but we all talk to him. He knows what we say," she said, leading the way to the street.

"How can he know what you say if he can't hear you?" Mandie insisted.

Lolly shrugged and said, "He knows. He just knows."

Mandie looked at Celia and rolled her eyes. This seemed to be a dead-end explanation. She thought the girl must be infatuated with Juan.

Celia smiled and said, "I believe we're headed for the park that we can see from our room."

Mandie looked ahead and agreed. "Yes, we are," she said. Turning to the maid, she asked, "Where does this park go?"

"Go?" Lolly asked in puzzlement.

"Yes, if we go through this park, where will we come out?" Mandie asked.

"Lots of things on other side of park," Lolly replied. Then turning to smile at Mandie, she said, "Ghosts live in the park at night. Never come here then."

"Ghosts? You believe in ghosts?" Mandie asked in surprise.

"Believe in ghosts?" Lolly questioned her as they entered the pathway through the park. "I know ghosts live here."

"How do you know ghosts live here?" Mandie asked.

"I see ghosts. I know ghosts when I see ghosts," Lolly insisted, glancing at Mandie with a deep frown.

Mandie was surprised at the girl's statement. "You've seen ghosts?" she questioned her. "What did they look like?"

Lolly frowned again and replied, "Different ghosts look different. I see different ghosts."

"Mandie, Senator Morton did say some people here believe in ghosts," Celia reminded her.

"Would you come back here with us after dark so we could see the ghosts, too?" Mandie asked the girl.

Lolly said, "Ghosts may not like you. You not from St. Augustine."

"Well, what would they do if they don't like us?" Mandie asked.

Lolly shrugged and said, "Do not know. Ghosts like me."

"Do the ghosts like Juan? Does he see ghosts in this park, too?" Mandie asked.

"Yes, big ghost with beard Juan see," Lolly said.

"How do you know that? Does he tell you that?" Mandie asked.

"Yes, he tell me," Lolly replied.

"Now, if he can't talk, how did he tell you that?" Mandie quickly asked, watching the girl closely.

"He . . . he tell me on paper," Lolly explained.

"On paper? You mean he writes it down?" Mandie asked.

"Yes, he write down," Lolly said and blew out a breath.

Mandie didn't believe the girl. She doubted that Lolly knew how to read and write. She would test her and see what happened.

Looking across the park, Mandie could see a Flagler Hotel sign. She put her hand on Lolly's arm to stop her and pointed at the sign. "Can you see that sign over there? What does it say? What's over there?"

"That is Flagler Hotel," Lolly immediately told her, smiling, and added, "Big place. Lots of people. Lots of money."

"Well, Mandie," Celia said, "that didn't work."

"No, but I'm not giving up," Mandie replied. She put Snowball down to walk at the end of his leash.

Mandie tried other places for Lolly to identify, but she knew every one of them. Evidently, she had everything memorized. They passed many beautiful buildings and eventually came to the other side of town. Then they turned back, and Lolly took them on different streets back to Senator Morton's house.

"Well, I'm tired now," Mandie said as they entered the front door. "Thank you, Lolly, for going with us."

Lolly smiled at her and continued down the hallway. The girls went up to their room.

"I suppose we have to change clothes to go down and eat tonight," Mandie said after putting Snowball down and unfastening his leash. "What will I put on? I didn't bring a whole lot of clothes with me."

"Oh, Mandie, you brought more than I did. I saw what you've got in the wardrobe," Celia said, going over to open its doors. She reached inside to sort through her dresses. Mandie stood behind her waiting to get to hers.

"Mandie, look!" Celia suddenly exclaimed as she stepped back to allow Mandie to look inside.

Mandie immediately saw that all their clothes had been turned the wrong way again. "I would like to know what's going on around here," she said.

"Who do you think is doing this?" Celia asked.

"I don't know," Mandie muttered impatiently as she began removing the clothes to turn them around. "It couldn't have been Juan, unless he did this while you and I and Lolly went out for a walk." Then she remembered the young man she had seen in the hallway when they first came but had not seen since. "I wonder who that man was I saw up here in the hallway that night," she added. "I haven't seen him again. Maybe he's the one doing all this. I'm going to find out just who this man is."

"I hope you can," Celia agreed, helping to rearrange the clothes.

"Just like I am going to find out who these so-called ghosts are in that park. You wait and see. I'll solve the whole thing. It may take a while, but I'll figure it all out."

Senator Morton's house was full of servants, and it could have been any one of them, but Mandie was determined to find the culprit.

Chapter 5 / Questions in the Dark

The day's events were discussed at the supper table that night. Mandie could hardly wait to inform the senator that Lolly believed in ghosts. Waiting for a lull in the conversation so she would have everyone's attention, the opportunity finally came.

Dessert and hot coffee had just been served and were the focal point of the adults' attention. Mandie laid down her fork on the side of the plate that held her slice of chocolate cake, cleared her throat, and looked at Senator Morton as she asked, "Did you know Lolly believes in ghosts? She took us through the park today and told us there were ghosts in there and that they liked her."

Senator Morton laughed as he replied, "I put nothing past Lolly. She has a very vivid imagination."

"Well, Senator Morton, are there really ghosts in that park?" Mandie asked, determined to pin him down for a yes or no answer.

"I can't rightfully say, since I don't believe in ghosts myself. I've always heard that if you don't believe in ghosts, then ghosts will never allow you to see them," he replied, picking up his coffee cup and then setting it back down. "Did Lolly tell you what kind of ghosts she sees in the park? What they look like, maybe?"

"No, sir, not really," Mandie replied as she tried to remember the exact remarks Lolly had made. Turning to Celia, she asked, "Lolly didn't describe the ghosts she claims live in the park, did she? Do you remember?"

"No, Mandie, I don't believe she did," Celia replied. "However, she did mention that there was a big ghost with a beard who Juan sees."

Senator Morton quickly laughed and said, "Juan believes in ghosts? I don't think so, even though Lolly said he did. Lolly lives in her own fantasy sometimes."

"Is Lolly in love with Juan?" Mandie asked with a big grin.

Mrs. Taft quickly caught her breath and spoke up. "Amanda, you shouldn't ask such questions. That is not your business."

"Yes, ma'am," Mandie said meekly and quickly concealed a smile.

"I can answer that for you, Miss Amanda," the senator said with a smile. "Lolly is in love with any man who will look her way. She was orphaned as a baby, and Maria raised her. But I'm afraid Maria never had children of her own and didn't exactly know what to do when Lolly grew up into a young woman who looks for love around every corner. I would say you shouldn't believe everything Lolly tells you."

"How do I know which part to believe, then?" Mandie asked, puzzled.

"After you've been around Lolly for a while, I'm sure you'll notice the glow that surrounds her when she is fantasizing and when she won't look you straight in the eye. That's when she is living in her own make-believe world."

"I will try to notice and remember," Mandie replied, picking up her fork to dig into the huge slice of chocolate cake. Then she thought of another question. Laying down the fork after one bite, she asked, "Senator Morton, can Juan hear at all? I mean, sometimes he seems to understand what we are saying."

"No, Juan can't hear a thing," Senator Morton told her, "unless it might be a loud explosion or something like that. I believe he did react to a cannon being fired in a celebration we had a while back, but he can't hear ordinary conversations."

"He seems to understand when someone stands directly in front of him and mouths the words," Celia put in.

"Yes, I believe sometimes he can understand part of it," the senator agreed.

"Senator Morton is having a small party tomorrow night, girls," Mrs. Taft told them. "Y'all should decide what you want to wear and hang it out to be pressed. I understand Maria will see to that."

Mandie immediately remembered the wardrobe. "Grandmother, Senator Morton, someone keeps coming into our room and turning our clothes the wrong way in the wardrobe. We hang them up all nice and neat, and when we come back to get something, they are all jumbled up and turned the wrong way."

"Oh dear," Mrs. Taft said with a sigh.

"Are you sure, Miss Amanda?" Senator Morton asked.

"Yes, sir, it has happened twice," Mandie told him.

"Yes, sir, it did," Celia added.

"I can't imagine what is going on, unless one of the maids slips in there to look at your beautiful clothes. Maybe that's what's happening," Senator Morton said thoughtfully. "I'll ask Maria to see that the maids do not go in your room unless you ask for them."

"But Juan has been in our room, too," Mandie quickly told him. "The other night when I went up there to take Snowball, I met him coming out of our room."

Senator Morton frowned and said, "I have no idea what Juan would be doing in your room, but you can rest assured I will find out. I'm sorry, and I'll see that it doesn't happen again."

"I didn't think you would be sending Juan up to our room when you have all these maids working here," Mandie told him.

"If it does happen again, please come directly to me," the senator said.

Mandie looked at Celia. She was really puzzled now. If the senator had not sent Juan to their room, and Juan knew he was not allowed in there, why was he in their room? She knew Celia could read the questions in her mind.

After a quiet evening in the parlor, everyone went to their rooms early. Mandie and Celia were not sleepy, and they knelt by the open window in their room to gaze out into the darkness and discuss the day's events.

"Mandie, do you believe Lolly really thinks she sees ghosts in the park over there?" Celia asked.

"She may just be teasing us with such stories," Mandie replied.

"But she claims Juan has seen a ghost, too, over there," Celia reminded her.

"Yes, and she said the ghosts might not like us because we are not from St. Augustine," Mandie replied. Suddenly she stood up and said, "Let's just go over there and see for ourselves what's in that park after dark. Want to go?" She looked down at her friend.

Celia rose and said, "Mandie, do you really want to go into that dark place? Couldn't we just walk through it again in the daytime?"

"But, Celia, the ghosts don't come out in the daytime," Mandie told her. "We have to go at night if we want to see them."

"Well, even at night we might not see any ghosts. Lolly may be just making all this up, you know," Celia argued.

"We could go find out," Mandie said. "Come on."

"Suppose we do see a real ghost, Mandie? What will we do?" Celia asked in a shaky voice.

"We will scare the ghost instead of letting it cause us to be afraid. Are you coming?" Mandie asked, walking toward the door of the room.

Snowball, who had been curled up and sleeping on the bed, rose, stretched, and loudly meowed at that moment.

"No, Snowball, you are not going this time, you hear? Just go right back to sleep," Mandie told the cat as she rubbed his head.

But Snowball was insistent. He meowed louder,

jumped down from the bed, and rubbed around Mandie's ankles.

"Are you going to take him?" Celia asked, watching from across the room. "Don't you think a cat might scare the ghosts away? I've heard tales about cats seeing things we can't see."

Mandie laughed and said, "I don't think Snowball could scare anyone away, but he is not going with us. I'll be sure we shut him up here in the room while we're gone," Mandie said, walking again toward the door. Looking back, she asked, "Are you coming, Celia? Let's hurry."

"I suppose I will go," Celia replied, slowly joining her at the door. "I just hope we don't see any real ghosts."

"There are no real ghosts, Celia. I promise you that," Mandie said, opening the door wide enough to step into the hallway. As Celia followed, Mandie quickly closed the door, shutting Snowball inside the room. Putting her finger on her lips to motion to Celia to be quiet, she tiptoed down the hallway toward the staircase.

The girls slowly descended into the front hallway below, and luckily none of the steps squeaked. Mandie led the way in the darkness directly to the front door. Everyone had gone to bed or to their rooms for the night, and the house was dark and quiet.

The moon was not shining, and Mandie felt her way into the yard. Suddenly she saw two men standing not ten feet from her, talking. She motioned to Celia, and they ducked behind some shrubbery. The man who was doing the talking was speaking in such a low voice and so softly that she couldn't understand his words. The other man seemed to be listening intently. Suddenly, from behind her, Celia stifled a sneeze, but not before she made a strange sound. Both men instantly straightened up and walked away—one went away from the house and the other man toward the house.

"Juan!" Mandie exclaimed softly when she saw him move out of the shadows and toward the front door, entering the house quickly.

Celia squeezed her hand. "It was Juan!" she whispered.

"Yes! Come, let's follow the other man. He's headed toward the park," Mandie whispered as she quickly led the way.

The girls darted behind bushes along the way as they tried to keep the man in sight. He quickly entered the park, but he went in a different direction from the way Lolly had taken them. He seemed to be cutting diagonally across it to the left.

Keeping her eyes on the man instead of what was along the way, Mandie suddenly became aware of the fact that they had entered a cemetery.

At the same time, Celia reached to grab her hand and whispered, "Mandie! We are in a graveyard!" She walked as close to Mandie as she could without stumbling over her own feet.

Mandie hissed at her to be quiet and hurried on following the man. She was trying to get close enough to see what the man looked like. When they came to some large tombstones, she quickly darted in and out between them to move closer. The man paused for a moment to wipe his nose with his handkerchief, and Mandie was so close, she almost collided with him. Practically dropping behind a tombstone, she watched, hoping he hadn't seen them.

The man cleared his throat and put his handkerchief back into his pocket.

Mandie clearly saw his face and noticed that he had a beard.

While the girls waited for the man to get far enough ahead so they could safely follow, the man suddenly disappeared right before their eyes. Mandie quickly looked around, trying to locate him. Was he the ghost Lolly mentioned? Where had he gone? There were several crypts near where they stopped, and this apparently gave him enough cover to disappear.

"Oh, where did he go?" Mandie whispered in Celia's ear as they quickly but quietly moved around in circles, trying to locate him.

"He just . . . evaporated—just like a g-g-ghost!" Celia replied in an almost tearful, shaky voice.

"Well, he had to go somewhere," Mandie declared, still searching among the graves and monuments.

"He's gone," Celia told her. "Gone."

The girls stopped to look around. They were near the edge of the cemetery.

"He just knew a quick way out of here, that's what," Mandie told Celia. "And that's probably the man Lolly saw with Juan, and she thought he was a ghost here in the cemetery or in the park that she talked about."

"Let's get out of here, Mandie!" Celia begged.

Suddenly Mandie heard voices coming toward them, and she motioned for Celia to drop down out of sight with her behind a huge monument. She almost held her breath as she waited for the owners of the voices to come closer.

Finally two figures emerged out of the shadows

and walked past their hiding place. Mandie watched and saw that it was a young girl and a young man, holding hands as they slowly walked.

"I heard that she's one of those mountaineers and probably doesn't know what to do with a set of silverware," the girl was saying, "but her grandmother is dripping in wealth, so my mother says we have to be nice to her tomorrow night."

"I heard that she is pretty, and so is her friend, so I look forward to meeting them," the boy replied. "Anyway, we have to go. After all, Mr. Morton is our senator."

Their voices faded away as they disappeared from sight. Mandie, shaking with anger, rose from her hiding place, as did Celia. They grasped each other's hands.

"Mandie—" Celia began.

"Yes, they were talking about us," Mandie interrupted. "It was just like they knew we were here listening! Just you wait until I meet them tomorrow night! I'll fix them!"

"What are you planning to do, Mandie?" Celia asked.

"I don't know yet, but I'll think of some way to get even with them," Mandie replied.

"Maybe if we just turn on all our charms and be real sweet and nice to them, that would get away with them better than by being aloof and cold, Mandie," Celia suggested. "You know, do good to evil."

Mandie sighed and said, "I'm not sure, but I will be ready for them when they do turn up at Senator Morton's house tomorrow night. I just wonder who they are that they can act so uppity." She stood there fuming.

"Mandie, don't you think we ought to go back to our room?" Celia asked.

"I suppose so," Mandie agreed. "I've had enough for the night." She turned and started walking back the way they had come. "But you know, Celia, that man we followed might just be the man Lolly thought was a ghost."

"You are probably right," Celia agreed, walking close to Mandie's side as they carefully avoided stepping over graves.

"We can come back tomorrow night," Mandie told her.

"No, Mandie. Remember, the party is tomorrow night. We couldn't just leave," Celia reminded her.

"All right, the next night, then," Mandie agreed.

The girls didn't see or hear anyone else as they returned to the house. The front door was unlocked, and they quietly entered and went back up to their room, tiptoeing up the staircase.

As soon as Mandie opened the door, she looked around for Snowball to prevent him from racing out of the room. But he didn't come to greet her, and he wasn't on the bed.

"Snowball!" Mandie called, looking around the room.

"I don't see him," Celia said as she helped search.

"Someone had to let him out because I know I closed the door," Mandie declared. "Come on. We'll have to search the house. We can't let him run loose all night."

The girls quietly looked throughout the house, but Snowball was nowhere to be found.

"We can't go in people's rooms," Mandie whispered to Celia. "Maybe he's in the kitchen. The door's closed, and I don't know whether anyone is in there or not, but we'd better check."

As soon as Mandie pushed the kitchen door open, Snowball came running out, loudly meowing. Mandie snatched him up. "Sh-h-h-h! You'll wake everybody up. Let's get back to our room before someone sees us."

Once inside their room, Mandie put Snowball down. He ran for the bed and curled up in the middle of it.

"Somebody let him out," Mandie said, walking around the room.

Celia went over to the wardrobe to get her night-clothes down from the hangers inside. She opened the double doors and stepped back as she said, "Just come and look! Someone has rearranged our clothes again!"

"Oh no!" Mandie said, rushing to look inside the wardrobe. She stomped her foot and said, "This has got to stop! I'm going to find out who is doing this."

"And we should find out *why* they are doing it," Celia added.

"You're right," Mandie said, beginning to re-arrange her clothes. "Why are they doing it? Just to upset us? Or just to look at all our clothes? I don't think I've missed anything, so they aren't stealing."

"Someone must have known we went out," Celia remarked as she put her clothes in order.

"But we didn't see anyone, so how did anyone know we went out?" Mandie asked. Then stopping to look at Celia, she said, "Do you suppose Juan saw us and pretended he didn't, and then he came up here and did this while we were gone?"

"He might have, but I wish whoever keeps doing

it would stop," Celia replied. "This is causing a lot of trouble."

As soon as they were finished rearranging the clothes, they went to sit by the window.

"You know, Celia," Mandie said, "I'm almost positive that boy and girl in the park knew we were in there. So how did they know? And who were they? Where do they live? Also, for what other reason would they have been in the cemetery at that time of the night?"

"If we find the answers to those questions, we'll solve the mystery," Celia agreed.

"Maybe someone is spying on us, but why?" Mandie asked thoughtfully. "I'll just be glad to get back home. But before I go home, I will solve this mystery."

She had no clue as to how to begin, but she would find the answers no matter what!

Chapter 6 / Party Plans

The next day everyone stayed at the house preparing for the party that night, except for a short walk in the afternoon.

Mandie kept thinking about the girl and boy in the park. She tried to decide how she would handle the situation when she met them. She wished she had Joe Woodard to discuss the matter with. Joe always had suggestions and sometimes good solutions to problems she got involved in.

"You know, Celia, maybe I should tell my grandmother about those snobs in the park last night. But if I do, I would have to admit that you and I were out alone that late, and she wouldn't like that," Mandie told her friend as they lounged about in their room that afternoon after the walk.

"Oh no, Mandie, we would really be in trouble if your grandmother knew we went out when we were supposed to be getting ready for bed," Celia replied, stretching her legs out in front of her as she sat in a big chair.

"I suppose we are guilty of doing something we shouldn't have done," Mandie agreed, "but if we hadn't gone into that cemetery, we never would have heard those remarks about us." She flopped onto another chair.

"Well, which is more important, then, slipping out at night or overhearing those crude people?" Celia asked. "I mean, would it be worth it to tell your grandmother what we did in order to let her know she is also being talked about by someone who is coming to the party and who is going to act nice and proper, when all the time they are secretly making fun of us?"

"I just don't know, but I do know that if my grandmother knew about this, she would get back at those people," Mandie said with a big smile. "Believe me, she would do something that would bring them down a notch or two."

"You are a lot like your grandmother, Mandie. More so than your mother," Celia told her.

"I know. My mother is so sweet and kindhearted, she wouldn't harm a fly," Mandie agreed. "She must have taken after her father, but I never knew him. I imagine my grandmother was the boss in the family, even though Grandfather was an important man—a senator like Senator Morton."

"Maybe we could speak to Senator Morton and ask him not to let your grandmother know we were out late at night," Celia suggested. "After all, these are his friends who are coming to the party, I suppose. That boy did say they had to come because Senator Morton is a senator, didn't he?"

"Yes, I wouldn't go to someone's party just because they are wealthy or important. I think that's a silly attitude," Mandie replied. "I just don't know whether to tell Senator Morton or not."

"He is sweet on your grandmother, Mandie, and probably wouldn't like someone talking about her or us that way," Celia reminded her.

"I know, but what could he do about it?" Mandie asked. "He couldn't say anything to them because he is a politician and he needs everyone's vote to stay in office."

"He might put this above getting a vote," Celia said. "In fact, I believe I remember hearing him say last summer on the ship that he would probably retire after this term. Do you remember something like that?"

"No, not that I can remember," Mandie replied. "I suppose he is getting old and probably worn out from traveling back and forth to Washington all the time."

"Do you think he might marry your grandmother someday? Then he would be your step-grandfather, Mandie," Celia said with a grin.

Mandie shrugged and said, "That would be fine with me. Then maybe Grandmother would have someone else to take along on all her journeys instead of me. However, I am not sure my grandmother would ever agree to marry him. And I believe the secret reason is that she dearly loved my grandfather."

Celia cleared her throat and asked with another grin, "Mandie, will you ever marry Joe?"

Mandie blew out her breath, got up to walk around the room, and then turned to look at her friend. "If anyone else had ever asked me that, I'd say go mind your own business." She paused and returned to her chair. "But since you asked the question, I'll tell you the truth. I just don't know. That would be a long time in the future, and lots of things can happen before I'd ever make a decision about getting married to anyone." Straightening up in her chair, she asked with a big smile, "How about you? Do you plan on marrying Robert someday?"

Celia blushed, and she didn't look directly at Mandie when she replied, "Oh, Mandie, Robert is just a good friend. I don't believe I've met my future husband yet. I'm only fourteen."

"I know that, but you started this," Mandie agreed. "Therefore, you must have had something on your mind. And, by the way, you know my mother was only sixteen when she ran away and married my father."

"So I've heard," Celia said. "According to Senator Morton, there will be several young people our age at the party tonight, so who knows what might happen? There may be someone who is not a snob."

"I'm not sure we'll be able to tell the good ones from the bad ones, so to speak," Mandie said. "I can't imagine putting on a false front like that to make people think you are friendly when you're not really."

"Well, are we going to tell the senator or your grandmother, both, or neither one?" Celia asked.

"I'll have to think about it," Mandie said. "The decision might be spontaneous when I see those two snobs face-to-face."

"You don't mean you would confront them right here in the senator's house at his party, do you?" Celia asked in horror. "That would be terrible, Mandie."

"I know," Mandie agreed. "Uncle Ned is always telling me to think first and then act, but sometimes I don't exactly remember. I wish he were going to be here." Then smiling at her friend, she added, "That would be a blow to those social snobs, wouldn't it? To find themselves at a party with a Cherokee Indian?"

"Everybody loves Uncle Ned, Mandie," Celia replied. "Even President McKinley invited him with us to the White House for his second inauguration."

"Yes, if people don't like Uncle Ned, I'd say there's something wrong with them," Mandie agreed. "And speaking of the President of the United States, remember that strange woman, Miss Lucretia Wham, was really working for him when she was following us and Jonathan around all over Europe. Do you suppose she is here in St. Augustine on business for the president?"

"I don't know, Mandie," Celia replied. "But since President McKinley died and President Roosevelt took over, things might have changed."

"I wish we could catch up with her," Mandie said.

"Maybe she'll be at the party tonight. Senator Morton acted like he knew something about her when you told him you thought we had seen her," Celia suggested.

"But he didn't seem to know much about where she was, so how could he have invited her to the party?" Mandie asked.

"Mandie, you know Miss Wham. She goes anywhere she pleases without being exactly invited," Celia reminded her.

"But she always darts in and out of crowds and places and never stays anywhere very long," Mandie replied. "Maybe she has been in contact with Senator Morton, and he could have invited her to the party then. I hope she does show up. I'd like to talk to her about some things."

"Like what?" Celia asked.

"Like, is Juan really deaf and dumb? Are there people in the park making like ghosts to scare outsiders like us away?" Mandie said.

"Well, I don't know how she would answer all those questions when she probably doesn't know anything about the people or this town," Celia said.

"Now, Celia, don't ever say that. Miss Wham knew everything about everybody and everything that was going on when she followed us around," Mandie reminded her friend.

A sharp rap on the door startled the girls, and they both jumped up and started in that direction. Mandie got there first and opened the door. Lolly was standing outside in the hallway and was holding the girls' dresses that had been pressed for the party.

"Come on in. I'll take mine," Mandie offered as she reached for the dress and stepped back, allowing the maid to enter the room.

Celia took her dress, and both girls started for the wardrobe to hang them up on the hooks on the outside of the doors.

"My dress looks nice. Thank you, Lolly," Mandie told her as she fluffed out the lacy frills on the blue silk dress that matched her blue eyes.

"So does mine, thank you," Celia added, surveying the bright green taffeta dress on the hanger she held.

As the two girls hung up the dresses outside the wardrobe, Lolly followed them across the room without speaking. Mandie turned around to look at her.

"Is there something else, Lolly?" Mandie asked, going back toward the chair she had been sitting in.

Lolly looked from Mandie to Celia and back again without saying a word. Celia returned to her chair and was about to sit down when the maid finally spoke.

"Just want to let you know, the ghosts from the park will be at the party tonight," Lolly said with a serious look on her face as she tossed back her long black hair.

"What are you talking about?" Mandie asked, still standing.

"I say, the ghosts in the park will be at the party at this house tonight," the girl repeated.

"Real ghosts, Lolly?" Celia asked.

"Yes, real, big ghost with beard and others," Lolly said.

"Lolly, there are no real ghosts," Mandie told her as the three of them stood there in the middle of the room.

"Yes, real, but you no see so you not know," Lolly argued with a big frown as she stomped her foot.

"Will I be able to see them tonight?" Celia asked.

"And how are we supposed to know who is a ghost and who is not?" Mandie asked impatiently.

"You will know," Lolly replied, starting toward the door.

Mandie hurried to get between the girl and the door. "Lolly, there are no real ghosts," she argued.

"Is too," the girl answered, stomping her foot. "You see real ghosts in park last night."

"In the park last night? How did you know we were in the park last night?" Mandie asked, surprised at this.

"Just know," Lolly said.

"Were you following us last night? What were you doing in the park last night? And that big fellow with the beard, he is not a ghost, he is a real man," Mandie told her quickly.

"No, you will see!" Lolly almost shouted at Mandie as she raced for the door, ran out, and disappeared down the hallway.

Mandie slowly closed the door, sighed loudly, and looked at Celia, who was standing by her chair. "Sounds like someone was following us last night," she said. "And if it was Lolly, I'm pretty sure she was not alone in that dark park at that time of night." She flopped down in her chair.

Celia sat down, too. "I wonder why anyone would follow us," she said.

At that moment Snowball, who had been peacefully sleeping in the middle of the bed, jumped down and came running to Mandie. She picked him up. "I suppose we woke you up, Snowball," she said, cuddling him in her arms. The white cat began purring loudly.

There was another knock at the door. It opened, and Mrs. Taft entered the room, carrying a large bag.

"Oh dear, I'm sorry girls, but this party tonight seems to be a masquerade ball. I didn't quite understand when the senator told me about it," Mrs. Taft said, walking over to the bed and upending the bag's contents onto the counterpane.

Mandie and Celia quickly followed.

"We are supposed to wear masks, Grandmother?'' Mandie asked as she looked at the pile on the bed.

"Yes, the guests will be masked, and this is the best I could get for you girls here at almost the last minute. Do y'all think it's possible to fix up some getup from all this?'' Mrs. Taft asked as she looked at them.

Mandie instantly thought of the girl and boy in the park the night before. They would be wearing masks, but she hoped she would be able to spot them from their voices. "Oh yes, ma'am, Grandmother, we'll use some of this stuff,'' she replied.

"This will be fun,'' Celia said, poking through the masks, ribbons, and scarves on the bed, and picking up a green and black mask. "This will match my dress.''

"If you can't coordinate enough things with the dresses you all had pressed, just select other dresses that will suit,'' Mrs. Taft said. "Now I must hurry back and see to mine.''

As Mrs. Taft started for the door, Mandie asked, "Grandmother, what will you be wearing?''

Mrs. Taft turned back to smile at her as she said, "Why, I'm going to wear my black taffeta with a little white hat to make me a Pilgrim.''

"A Pilgrim?'' Mandie asked.

"Yes, a Pilgrim. Remember, we are descended from the Pilgrims,'' Mrs. Taft said as she went out the door.

"Mandie, how are we going to recognize anyone if everyone is wearing a mask?'' Celia asked.

"That's going to be fun, because we will be wearing masks, too. So it will take everyone a while to figure out who we are,'' Mandie said.

"As long as we don't talk,'' Celia cautioned her.

"Otherwise, they will know we do not have the familiar voices of their friends."

"You're right," Mandie agreed. She stood in the middle of the floor thinking for a moment, and then she said, "I think I'll wear something other than that blue dress. Then even Lolly won't know for sure who I am."

"Good idea!" Celia agreed.

Both girls went to the wardrobe and looked through their clothes.

"I have this white dress I haven't worn here," Mandie said, taking it down from the hanger.

"I have a black one with me," Celia said, reaching for hers. "Why don't we dress like ghosts, you in white for a good ghost and me in black for a bad ghost."

Mandie looked at her and laughed. "Are there supposed to be such things, Celia?"

"I don't know. I just made that up," Celia replied, shaking out the skirt of her black dress. "With all the talk around this town about ghosts, I thought we might as well make use of it."

"Maybe we can get Lolly to believe in us," Mandie said, laughing as she hung the white dress on a hook outside the wardrobe.

"We may scare Lolly." Celia giggled.

"I wonder where Grandmother got all that stuff she brought us," Mandie said, going back to look through the pile.

"Maybe Senator Morton keeps a stock of such things on hand for the parties he gives," Celia suggested, laughing as she joined Mandie.

The girls planned and sorted out the adornments. Snowball jumped up on the bed and tried to help.

"Mandie, why don't you take Snowball to the party? You could keep him on the leash," Celia suggested. "He's white, and you'll have on a white dress. You could decorate him to match your things."

Mandie thought about that for a moment and finally said, "I suppose I could. And if he gets out of control, I can always bring him back up here and shut him in our room." Then she smiled as she thought about it and added, "That might be a good idea. Maybe everyone will think he is a ghost cat."

"I doubt that," Celia replied with a grin.

"I'm really getting interested in this party now. Everyone will be wondering who everybody else is," Mandie said. "But I believe I will be able to identify the girl and boy in the park by their voices, no matter how much decoration they put on themselves."

"I could, too," Celia agreed.

"I might even do something mean while I'm undercover, and before they find out who I am, like acting as though I'm a royal princess or something. That will put an end to that girl's definition of me as a mountaineer who doesn't even know how to use silverware," Mandie declared, twirling around the room with a white silk scarf.

Mandie decided this party was going to be fun after all. She loved mysteries, and all the guests, including her and Celia, would be wearing mysterious outfits. And how nice it was going to be when she finally let the boy and girl know who she was. That would be a great satisfaction.

Chapter 7 / A-partying

Mandie and Celia experimented the rest of the afternoon with the costume accessories Mrs. Taft had brought them. Finally they were dressed and ready five minutes before it was time to go downstairs for the party.

Mandie stood before the full-length mirror in the corner of their room to check her appearance. She carefully adjusted the white scarf she had tied around her head to hide her hair and then smoothed the rouge she had put on her cheeks and lips. She had tied more scarves around her waist to make her skirt fluffier.

"I don't believe anyone would recognize me if they knew me," Mandie said. "And I don't know any of the guests coming for the party."

"Even I would doubt you are Mandie Shaw," Celia said with a laugh as she adjusted her mask.

"Before I put on my mask I need to tie the bow on Snowball's collar," Mandie said. She turned to the cat on the bed and said, "Come here, Snowball. We are going a-partying, and you need some kind of costume. I'm going to put a nice big white bow on your collar." As she talked she picked up the bow from the table nearby and began looping ribbons around the cat's collar. Snowball squirmed and meowed, plainly not liking what she was doing.

"I'll hold him for you, Mandie," Celia offered as she grasped the cat to hold him still.

Mandie got the bow tied on, but the minute the girls let go of him, Snowball began rolling and trying to rub off the decoration.

"Snowball, you are ruining the bow. Quit that," Mandie demanded as she picked him up and stood him upright to fasten on his leash.

Snowball growled angrily and managed to escape. He ran across the room, trying to shake off the bow, and then rolled on the floor.

Mandie sighed as she watched him and said, "All right, Snowball, you can't go to the party if that's the way you're going to behave. Come here. I'll take the bow off." She captured him and removed the bow. He immediately ran under the bed, meowing furiously.

"I wouldn't bother with him anymore, Mandie," Celia told her. "Leave him here. You don't really need him to support your act."

"I'll have to bring him something to eat later, since we are having supper served during the party," Mandie said. She hurried to put on her mask and then said, "Come on. Let's go downstairs before any of the servants come up here to get us. If we mingle with the guests, maybe Lolly and the others won't recognize us."

"Good idea," Celia agreed, fluffing out the gathers in her long black skirt as she followed Mandie to the door.

When they got down to the last landing, Mandie could hear voices in the parlor down the hall. "Come on. Let's go out the side door and come in the front so everyone will think we are guests, too. Hurry!" She ran to the outside door, which opened out onto a patio. Celia followed.

Several carriages stood in the driveway, and people in costume were walking toward the front door.

Mandie put her hand out to stop Celia and said, "Wait. Let's go in right behind that couple with the walking canes. We can probably slip past them without anyone noticing us."

The girls stayed near the bushes until the couple entered the front door, then they quickly stepped inside without being noticed by Senator Morton or Mrs. Taft, who were greeting the guests. They walked on across the large parlor to a corner where no one was standing at the moment.

Mandie felt her heartbeat quicken as she closely watched the guests arriving in a steady stream. Evidently everyone believed in being prompt to the minute. And her grandmother had said this would be a small party. Why, a hundred guests must have entered the parlor since she and Celia had come down. She was keeping an eye out for the girl in the park. She didn't think she would recognize her because it had been so dark in the graveyard and everyone at the party was in costume and masked. But she believed if she listened closely to the bits of conversation around her she would be able to identify the girl's voice.

"What are you going to do if you see that girl?"

Celia asked in a whisper behind her hand.

"I'm not sure yet," Mandie murmured back with a frown as she thought about it. Should she walk up to the girl and announce, "I'm that mountaineer from North Carolina who doesn't know how to use silverware"? No, she was sure the girl had planned her speech last night knowing that Mandie was nearby. She could just turn her nose up and ignore the girl. Then again, she might put on a foreign accent as she remembered the speeches of the various countries she had visited with her grandmother and Celia during the previous summer.

After a while it seemed that all the guests had arrived, and Mandie was suddenly aware of her grandmother coming in her direction. She whispered to Celia, "Can we fool Grandmother?"

"I don't think so," Celia mumbled back.

Mrs. Taft walked right up to Mandie and said, "Amanda, you and Celia should mingle with the guests."

"Oh, Grandmother, we didn't fool you for a minute, did we?" Mandie replied with a sigh. "Everyone else is masked, so how can we mingle with the guests when we don't know who is who?"

"That's the fun of a masked party," Mrs. Taft said. "You talk to everyone, and then when the masks come off later, you are usually surprised at whom you were talking with. Now move on around the room instead of just standing there." She turned to go back toward the guests she had been talking with.

Mandie looked at Celia and said, "I suppose we have to. But tell me how Grandmother knew who we were, with all this getup. Do you suppose everyone else will figure it out, too?"

"Mandie, your grandmother gave us all these scarves and masks we've got on. Of course she would know who we are," Celia reminded her.

"You're right," Mandie agreed, looking at the costumed people moving about. "Come on. We might as well get this over with. Help me look for that boy and girl in the park last night, and if you recognize them, start coughing to alert me."

"All right, but you do the same thing so I'll know, too, if you spot them first," Celia agreed.

Mandie straightened the scarf around her head and led the way into the crowd. The parlor was full, the library was full, and the huge dining room was overflowing with people. Mandie tried to avoid looking directly at anyone in order to keep from having to enter into a conversation, and no one seemed to pay any attention to Mandie and Celia as they slowly walked through the rooms.

"Mandie, let's find someplace to sit down and just watch for a little while," Celia suggested as they entered the library.

"But, Celia, Grandmother told us to mingle with the guests, remember?" Mandie said as they passed an elderly couple who were not dressed in costumes but were wearing masks. After they walked by the couple, Mandie glanced back at them and was surprised to see the woman also turning to look at her and Celia. The woman had probably figured out who the girls were. Mandie quickened her pace. "Come on. Let's go on into the dining room and then circle back to the parlor," she told Celia.

Just as they got to the door of the dining room, a couple dressed like turtles stopped them.

"I say, there," a male voice said in an improvised British accent from behind a dark mask, "would it be that you two are the guests of our host?"

"Yes, I do believe they are," a young female voice added from the second turtle.

Mandie looked at the padded costumes the two had on and wondered how they could stand such stuff in the hot weather. Their outfits were designed to look as though the turtles were walking on their hind legs, and she doubted that real turtles could do that. Why didn't the people just wear some kind of normal costume? She decided they were not the couple in the park last night.

"Yes, my name is Mandie Shaw, and this is my friend Celia Hamilton," Mandie told them.

"How do you do?" Celia said to the strangers.

"I am Rickard Bernadine, and this is Eleanor Morton," the male voice replied.

"Morton? Related to Senator Morton?" Mandie asked, smiling at the girl.

"Yes, he is my uncle, my father's brother," Eleanor explained. "I am glad to make your acquaintances. I have heard lots about you two from my uncle."

Mandie grinned and asked, "And was it partly bad things?"

"Oh no, quite the contrary," Eleanor said. "He speaks highly of you and Celia and of your families, especially your grandmother, Mandie." She also grinned.

Mandie and Celia looked at each other and smiled.

"So other people notice besides us," Mandie said.

"That my uncle is quite smitten with your grandmother?" Eleanor asked. "Yes, he is, and most everyone knows it."

"Do you think that one day your grandmother will become Mrs. Morton?" Rickard asked.

"That's what Celia and I talk about sometimes. I don't know," Mandie told her new friends. "I do know that she was deeply in love with my grandfather, according to everyone who knows her. He died before I was born, so I didn't know him, but Grandmother has told me that my grandparents and Senator Morton and his wife were close friends for years and years."

"Do y'all live here in St. Augustine?" Celia asked.

"No, Rickard is from Savannah, where I live, but his family moved to Jacksonville last year," Eleanor explained.

"Where do y'all go to school?" Celia asked.

The two turtles looked at each other and smiled.

"We have been out of school for quite a while now," Eleanor explained. "You see, we are both twenty-two years old."

Mandie gasped in surprise. "I can't tell with all the makeup and costumes y'all have on, but I thought y'all were probably around our ages. I will be fourteen in June, and Celia was fourteen in March. We go to school in Asheville, North Carolina, at the Misses Heathwood's School for Girls."

"Yes, I know," Eleanor replied. "My uncle mentioned it."

"I understand food will be served shortly, and yes, there are the servants bringing in the food right now," Rickard said, motioning inside the dining room, where they had stopped near the doorway.

"Some of these people are going to have trouble

eating with those masks covering their faces," Mandie said, grinning. "Let's watch and see how they do it."

"We aren't supposed to take off our masks until midnight, so maybe those in that shape will wait until midnight to eat," Eleanor said.

Mandie looked back into the room they were leaving and caught her grandmother's eye. Mrs. Taft motioned for them to move on and circulate among the guests, and Mandie understood what she was signaling to them.

"Your grandmother is telling us to move on again, Mandie," Celia said as she, too, saw the motions.

"Right," Mandie agreed. She turned to the two turtles and said, "I'm glad to have met y'all, and I'll catch back up with you later, but my grandmother keeps watching us and insists we circulate among everybody."

"She's right," Eleanor agreed. "Everyone wants to meet y'all. We'll see y'all later."

"And when you two get tired of circulating, just find us in the crowd and we'll go take a break in a corner somewhere," Rickard told the girls.

"Thanks," Mandie and Celia both said as they moved on into the dining room, heading for the door to the hallway as the servants began placing large bowls of food on the long table.

As Mandie and Celia hurried out into the hallway from the dining room, they almost collided with Juan, who was walking in their direction.

Mandie stopped short, took a deep breath, closed her eyes, and looked directly at the man. "I'm sorry, we got in too big a hurry," she apologized as Juan stepped aside to avoid a collision.

Juan looked at her, smiled, and continued on his way down the hall. Mandie turned to Celia and said, "He was coming from the direction of the staircase. I wonder if he's been up in our room again?"

"Well, it's too late now to catch him in the act. After we eat, we can take food to Snowball and look around our room," Celia told her.

"Yes, and for right now, let's see if we can find the girl and the boy from the park last night," Mandie replied, leading the way back down to the parlor.

Mandie could feel the people in the parlor turning to look at her and Celia. Evidently they were aware now of their identifications in spite of the costumes and masks. But she and Celia did not know these people and that put them at a disadvantage. As she and Celia continued across the room, she noticed a beautiful young girl about her age with long curly dark hair and no disguise except a small shiny mask over her eyes. She was wearing a long, full-skirted dress of red taffeta and had a thin black silk scarf around her shoulders. The boy with her wore the latest fashion in clothes and had donned only a small mask for the party. His hair was also black and curly.

When Mandie and Celia started to walk past the two, the girl immediately looked at them and asked, "Are you having fun in our town? St. Augustine must be quite different from the place you live."

Mandie immediately turned to look closely at the two. Celia started coughing suddenly. The alarm sounded in Mandie's head. That was their signal if they found the couple from the park. And yes, these two could be the culprits.

Mandie quickly decided on her strategy. Stopping and looking directly at the girl, she replied in what she would have called her most highfalutin voice, "I do beg your pardon. Were you addressing us?" She watched for the girl's reaction, which was one of surprise and puzzlement.

Celia, who was at Mandie's side, gave a little tug to Mandie's sleeve and whispered, "Let's go."

Mandie ignored Celia and continued with her conversation. "I do believe I asked you a question," Mandie insisted, staring at the girl.

The girl seemed to be unable to speak as Mandie continued. "We did see you two in the park last night, you know."

The girl quickly drew a deep breath, looked at the boy with her, and finally replied, "If we were in the park and you saw us, then you were also in the park."

The boy with her said, "That's right. You can't deny that."

"Oh, you two are the most impossible people I have ever met!" Mandie exclaimed, keeping her put-on accent.

"And I say the same for you two," the girl told her. Turning to the boy with her, she said, "Let's go get our food, Ted." She took the boy's arm, and they quickly walked off into the room on their way to the dining room.

Celia stomped her foot and looked at Mandie as they watched the two disappear in the crowd. "Mandie, I was not coughing to let you know that those two looked like the two in the park last night. I coughed because a man passed by who was smoking a cigar."

Mandie looked at her friend and exclaimed, "Oh no! What have I done! There's no telling who those two people are. They may be good friends of Senator Morton, or my grandmother even. This is going to cause a catastrophe, Celia. If this gets back to Grandmother, I know very well what will happen. She will be furious. I'll never hear the end of it. Oh, what can I do?"

"There's nothing you can do, Mandie. It's all done," Celia replied. "Don't you think we'd better move along in the crowd?"

"Yes, I suppose," Mandie agreed as the two walked slowly on.

"I'm sorry, Mandie, if you thought that was the signal," Celia explained, "but that man came right by me, just puffing and puffing on his stinky old cigar, and it made me cough."

"It's not your fault I made a fool of myself. I should have talked to the girl and the boy to see what they had to say before I tried anything," Mandie said, nervously glancing around the crowd to see where her grandmother was. She hoped to avoid Mrs. Taft for the rest of the evening just in case the report of her unladylike behavior circulated to her grandmother.

They kept moving around and finally got in line to get food from the long dining table. They took their well-filled plates and found a small nook in the corner of the library that was unoccupied and sat down on stools to eat. Tall plants in huge pots shielded them from view as other people moved in and out of the room.

Mandie was afraid to talk for fear someone would hear her and come join them. She didn't want any company while she silently ate her food, and she was so upset she couldn't have told you what the food was. Celia also refrained from conversation. Finally they had finished their food and saved the scraps for Snowball.

Mandie said in a low voice, "I suppose I should go take some food to Snowball, don't you think?"

"Yes, I'll go with you," Celia replied.

As the girls started to rise, they heard voices come into the room, just out of view because of the plants. "Did you see her absolutely cut down Bonnie and Ted? Bonnie said she has the most vile temper," the girl was saying.

Mandie immediately recognized the voice as that of the girl in the park the night before. She froze and did not move. She was not going to get into more trouble than she had already created. Maybe the girl and boy would leave the room, and she and Celia could get out. She looked at her friend and saw that she had also recognized the voice.

"Bonnie can have a so-called vile temper herself sometimes, if I remember correctly," the boy said.

"Oh, George, all girls have a little temper sometimes," she said.

"I know you do, Thelma Coty," the boy said. "All Cotys do."

"Don't forget that includes you. You are my cousin, you know. Even if it is about the thirteenth, you have some of the same blood, George Tollison," the girl replied.

"I know, I know," George said. "Which is a lucky thing for me. I can only escort you around when you run out of friends because I'm your cousin. But that means I can also look at other girls, and I think I would like to meet those two girls."

"Come on, let's see if we can spot them," Thelma said.

Mandie and Celia listened quietly as the other two left the room. Both girls held on to their plates with the food left for Snowball. Then Mandie whispered, "Let's get out of here, fast." She hurried through the room and out the door into the connecting hallway at the side of the house.

"Mandie, where are you going?" Celia asked, following her.

"I think we can get up to our room from an outside staircase this way. Let's go see," Mandie told her. "Please don't spill the rest of your food."

As the two rushed up the outside staircase, Celia remarked, "Mandie, we never did get a look at those two, so we won't know them if we see them again."

"All we have to do is listen. I'll recognize them," Mandie said, stopping to turn back to her friend as she added, "but, Celia, I'm not going to say anything to them. I'll just ignore them. I don't want to cause more trouble than I have already."

"That's a good decision," Celia agreed.

When they finally found the way to their room through the outside balconies, Mandie opened the door and called to Snowball, "Come on, Snowball. We've brought you some food." She quickly looked around. There was no sign of the white cat.

"Mandie, I believe he's gone," Celia told her as she searched for him.

Mandie finally stood up and said, "Yes, someone has let him out. Oh, this is going to be a job finding him with all those people downstairs."

"I wonder who let him out?" Celia remarked, placing her plate on the bureau.

Mandie looked at her, rushed over to the wardrobe, opened the doors, and inspected their clothes.

Everything seemed to be the way they had left it.

"Well, at least someone didn't come in here and turn our clothes all around again," Mandie said, closing the doors to the huge piece of furniture.

"No, but someone had to have let Snowball out because we were sure we closed the door, remember?" Celia said.

"I know," Mandie agreed. With a big sigh, she asked, "Where do you think we should start looking?"

"Oh, Mandie, I have no idea," Celia replied.

"At home he heads for the kitchen when he gets out of my room. Maybe that's where he is now," Mandie suggested. "Maybe he smelled food and was hungry. Let's see if we can find the way to the kitchen without going back downstairs through the guests. We ought to be able to go down the outside stairs and find an entrance in the back somewhere."

"Yes, lead the way. I'm right with you," Celia agreed.

The girls went back down the outside stairs. They practically ran into Juan at the bottom of the steps. Evidently he was in a hurry and was going up. Mandie sighed and quickly moved to one side out of his way. He smiled at the girls and rushed up the stone steps.

"I wonder where he was going in such a hurry," Mandie remarked as she led the way around the house, looking for an entrance to the kitchen.

"Our room, maybe?" Celia asked.

Mandie stopped to look back at her friend and said as she stomped her foot, "Well, I just can't go two directions at one time. I'll have to find Snowball first, and then I'll see if we can find out where Juan was going."

This party was causing a lot of hassle for Mandie. She would be glad when the guests said goodbye and things settled back down for the night, at least. In the meantime, her beloved white cat could be just about anywhere. She had to find him.

Chapter 8 / Who Is Who?

Mandie and Celia finally located an outside door in the back of the mansion that they thought would lead to the kitchen. Mandie opened it, and they found themselves staring down a long, dark hallway. The girls stood still to look around. There were several closed doors.

"I believe I smell food that way," Mandie said, pointing down the corridor to the last door on the left.

"Yes," Celia agreed.

They walked down the hallway to the door they had decided upon, and just before they reached it, the door suddenly opened and someone rushed out into the hallway in their direction. The girls stopped in their tracks.

"It's Lolly," Mandie said, and quickly turning to Celia, she asked, "Do you think she'll recognize us?"

"Probably," Celia instantly responded.

Lolly did recognize them immediately. She came to stand in front of them and said, "You must be lost. Party is in front of house."

"We know that, but my cat has disappeared out of our room, and we thought maybe he had headed for the kitchen for food," Mandie explained.

"Sí, cat is in kitchen eating," Lolly explained, turning to go on her way.

"Wait," Mandie said. "Do you know how he got out of our room and into the kitchen?"

"Do not know. Only came to door and Cook let him in. Now I have errand to get to," Lolly said, continuing down the hallway toward the outside door.

"Well, maybe Cook will know how he got down here. Come on," Mandie said to her friend.

Walking up to the door through which Lolly had come, Mandie slowly pushed it open and was greeted with strong food odors and loud, fast talking between the servants inside the kitchen. No one noticed the two girls standing there.

"Snowball!" Mandie called loudly over the hustle and bustle in the room.

The noise and conversation were immediately turned off, and everyone stopped to stare at Mandie and Celia.

Mandie, feeling uncomfortable with all the attention pointed at them, quickly said, "My cat, Snowball, is not in our room. Is he down here?"

"Oh, sí, sí" was repeated around the room.

An older woman in a more sophisticated uniform, which Mandie thought must make her the boss, spoke to Mandie. "Cat hungry. We feed. He eat good," she said, pointing to Snowball, whom Mandie now saw gobbling down the food on a plate under the table. The woman shook her head and added, "Not good when cat get hungry. Must feed or cat get too thin."

"Yes, I know. Thank you all," Mandie said, going to stoop down by her cat. "Hurry, Snowball, so we can take you back up to our room."

Snowball looked up at his mistress with his blue eyes, meowed loudly, and quickly returned to his food.

The woman watched and then spoke again. "Cat stay here. You party. Back later," she said. "Bella watch. You go."

"Thank you, Miss Bella," Mandie said. "We'll be back soon."

As the girls turned to leave the kitchen, Bella suddenly clapped her hands and called out to the other help. "Work! Get work done! Now!"

The noise and conversation began again as the girls left the room. Outside in the hallway, Mandie blew out her breath and said, "I don't think I would like working for Bella."

"Neither would I," Celia agreed. "Now what do we do?"

"I suppose we have to go back to the party," Mandie said with a long groan, and then quickly added, "Let's go check our room before we do. Hurry."

She rushed to the outside door and ran up the outside staircase. Celia followed right behind her. Slowing down in the upstairs hallway, Mandie put her finger to her lips to motion for Celia to be quiet. They slipped along the corridor to the door of their room. Then Mandie quietly, slowly turned the doorknob and eased the door open.

"No one is here right now," Mandie said, entering the room and looking around. Everything seemed to be exactly the way they had left it. "Let's check the wardrobe," she added and ran to open its doors.

Celia came right behind her and watched as Mandie examined their clothes hanging inside. "Nothing bothered this time," she said.

"No, everything seems to be the way we hung it," Mandie agreed, closing the doors to the wardrobe. "Now we have to get back downstairs before Grandmother misses us. And I hope that girl I spoke to and her friend Ted have not spread any talk about that. We'll soon know."

When the girls slipped back among the crowd in the parlor, no one seemed to notice. Mandie glanced around for the turtle-costumed couple but could not see them. As she and Celia walked on through the parlor, Mandie suddenly spotted her grandmother across the room and gasped when she realized who was talking to the lady. The girl and boy she had had words with seemed to be in a deep conversation with Mrs. Taft.

"Oh no," Mandie murmured to Celia. "Look who's talking to Grandmother." She darted between a group of tall people nearby in an effort to keep from being seen. "Let's go in the other room," she whispered to Celia.

The crowd she was hiding behind suddenly moved on in separate ways, and when she glanced at her grandmother again, Mrs. Taft had seen her and Celia. She was motioning for them to come over to her.

"Here we go," Mandie muttered to Celia as she slowly began making her way through the crowd toward her grandmother. Celia followed.

The girls were halfway across the room when

Senator Morton suddenly appeared before them with a big smile. "I was trying to intercept your path, Miss Amanda and Miss Celia. I have some friends I'd like y'all to meet," he said.

"Yes, sir," Mandie replied. "I'd like to meet your friends."

"So would I, sir," Celia added.

"Let's see if we can work our way through here," the senator told them as he moved toward the other side of the room.

Mandie was too short to see where Senator Morton was leading them, but when she finally got a view through the crowd, she gasped to herself. Senator Morton seemed to be leading them directly toward her grandmother, who was still talking with the young girl and boy. And she suddenly knew the senator's friends would be that young couple. What was going to happen? She glanced at Celia, who nodded to show she understood, too.

Finally reaching Mrs. Taft, the senator made the introductions. "Miss Amanda, Miss Celia, I would like for you to meet Miss Bonnie Sammons and young Mr. Ted Tilden."

Mandie was amazed to hear the girl say, "How do you do? It's a pleasure to meet you."

And the young man added, "Yes, it is a great pleasure to meet both you young ladies."

"How do you do?" Mandie was finally able to say.

"Pleasure to meet you both," Celia chimed in with ladylike dignity.

"Amanda, Bonnie's grandmother and I were old school chums long ago," Mrs. Taft said. "I had lost touch, but Bonnie tells me her grandmother passed away about ten years ago."

Mandie was puzzled by the whole situation and could think of nothing to say. What was going on here? She quickly decided she must have been right when she thought the couple were the same ones who had been in the park doing all that talking. She remembered the girl had said she would have to be nice to Mandie because of Mrs. Taft's wealth. Well, if Bonnie Sammons wanted to play a game, she would play right along with her until she got a chance to show the girl up for what she was like underneath all this courtesy.

Celia stood by listening. Looking at Mandie, she said under her breath, "I don't believe you made a mistake after all."

Mandie grinned at her and nodded.

"Bonnie's grandmother was also an old friend of mine, and I just wanted you girls to become acquainted," Senator Morton said, glancing around the group. "And Ted's grandparents were slightly connected to my wife's family by marriage. Even though many people have moved here from up north in the last few years, we still have our old friends, although they are getting fewer every year."

"So who are you related to, Mandie?" Ted asked, surprising Mandie. He smiled at her.

"I'm related to everyone that my grandmother is related to," Mandie replied, not quite sure how to handle this conversation.

"That's on your mother's side," Ted said. "I hear tell you have some Cherokee connections."

"Oh yes, my mother is Grandmother's daughter. But my father's mother was full-blooded Cherokee," Mandie told him.

"Which makes you one-fourth Cherokee," Bonnie added.

"But you don't look like an Indian, with that blond hair and blue eyes," Ted told her.

Mandie frowned, trying to decide whether he was being critical of her ancestry. "But I am one-fourth, and I am proud of it. That's what God made me," she said, straightening her shoulders and looking him in the eye.

"Excuse me, Ted," Bonnie said, quickly waving to someone across the room. "I see the Stones motioning for us to come over there. Remember, we promised to spend some time with them tonight." Turning to Mrs. Taft and Mandie and Celia, she added, "If y'all will please excuse us, we will try to catch up with you later. Nice meeting you, Mandie and Celia." She put on a brilliant smile.

"I'm glad to have met y'all," Mandie said, not to be outdone with her politeness.

"Yes, it was nice," Celia added.

As soon as Bonnie and Ted got out of hearing distance, Mrs. Taft said, "Well, Amanda, I take it you were not interested in really becoming acquainted with those two."

"Well, Grandmother," Mandie began slowly, and then looking directly at her grandmother, she added, "They were too formal, too stilted. I don't think they were really interested in meeting us, either. They're not my kind of people."

"Why, Amanda, what in the world do you mean by that, not your kind of people?" Mrs. Taft asked, moving over near a tall potted plant to get out of the flow of traffic.

"Pardon me, but I believe I know exactly what Miss Amanda is saying," Senator Morton spoke up.

"Those two young people acted stuffy and too uppity. I caught that immediately. I'm sorry you are not going to be friends, but their elders were a completely different kind of people—friendly, down-to-earth, and really good friends with your grandmother and me. I just don't understand your generation sometimes, Miss Amanda."

"Please, let's not get into that," Mrs. Taft quickly spoke up. "We made an effort, since their families were old friends of ours, but let it go at that. You girls, move on around the room and get acquainted with other people. Enjoy yourselves."

"Yes, ma'am," Mandie said, grinning that her grandmother usually understood her so well.

Mandie and Celia continued moving through the crowd. Several people stopped them to introduce themselves. The girls didn't see the turtle-costumed couple again. Finally midnight came, and everyone unmasked, but there were no surprises because the girls didn't recognize any of the guests.

"I haven't seen Bonnie and Ted again, have you?" Mandie asked as they stood by the doorway to the hall.

"Yes, I saw them leave with those people they called the Stones. I suppose they had more interesting things to do," Celia replied.

When the rooms were finally empty, the girls told Mrs. Taft and Senator Morton good-night.

"Be sure you girls go straight to your room and stay there, now. It's too late to go wandering around anywhere," Mrs. Taft told them in the parlor.

"Yes, ma'am, we will," Mandie told her. "I'm really tired. We have to get Snowball from the kitchen, and then we'll go upstairs. Good night."

Mandie and Celia hurried down the inside hallway this time to the kitchen. The room was full of servants and noise as the cleanup after the party progressed. Bella saw them when they entered.

"Lolly take cat upstairs," Bella called to them. "Good night." She turned to her duties.

"Well, all right. Thank you, Miss Bella," Mandie replied. She and Celia hurried back into the hallway and up the stairs to their room.

"I'm glad to see Snowball is really here this time," Mandie said as she opened the door and found the white cat curled up on the big bed.

"Me too," Celia agreed, pulling the ribbon out of her long auburn curls. "I believe I'll fall asleep the minute I get in that bed."

"You mean without even discussing all those people at the party?" Mandie teased, unfastening the bodice of her dress and preparing for bed. "Why, I figured we had lots to talk about."

"Oh, Mandie, can't it wait till morning?" Celia said with a big yawn as she removed her party dress.

"I suppose so," Mandie said, walking over to the wardrobe and opening the doors to get her night-clothes down. She glanced up at the hangers, stomping her foot. "Celia, the hangers are mixed up again." She let out a long, loud sigh.

"Maybe it was Lolly. Bella said she brought Snowball up here," Celia reminded her. "Anyhow, I'm too sleepy to bother. I'm going to bed." She quickly pulled down her nightclothes and hung up the dress she had worn.

"All right," Mandie agreed.

Within a few minutes the girls were ready for bed. They jumped under the sheets and said good-night to each other.

Soon Mandie could hear Celia's breathing rhythm change and knew Celia was asleep, but she couldn't go to sleep herself. She got up silently and went over to sit in the window and look out. The moon was shining, but most of the buildings in the distance were dark. The townspeople had gone to bed.

Curled up there in the big chair, a million thoughts ran through Mandie's head. She thought about the party, and about Bonnie and Ted, whom she was sure were the ones she and Celia had seen in the park. She wondered where Eleanor and Rickard, the "turtles," had gone, because she believed they left the party early. Then there was Juan. Where was he right now? Was he the one who had been in their room?

"Oh shucks!" Mandie murmured to herself as the mysteries swirled around in her head. "I need Joe to help me figure things out."

And Joe Woodard, what was he doing right now? Would he be able to take some vacation from college and come back home while she was out of school for the summer? She missed him and didn't like the idea that he was so far away. Never in their lives had they been so far apart.

Mandie slowly drifted off to sleep in the chair. She was suddenly awakened by a thud in her lap and straightened up to find Snowball there. She rubbed her eyes and yawned.

Looking around the room, Mandie realized she had been dreaming of home. And she didn't like what she had dreamed. She had plainly seen Joe Woodard arm in arm with a beautiful brunette, who was smiling happily at him. Mandie had been trying to find him in a maze of rooms and watched as the two walked by. Joe didn't seem to see or hear her when she called to him. He kept his eyes on the brunette and disappeared into the next room.

"My goodness!" Mandie exclaimed to herself. "That was a stupid dream, or was it? How do I know what Joe Woodard is doing down there in New Orleans at that college?"

Mandie put Snowball down and stood up and stretched. She walked over to the bed and saw that Celia was still sleeping.

"It doesn't really matter because it was all a dream," Mandie muttered to herself as she climbed quietly back into bed. "I'll sort it all out tomorrow."

Chapter 9 / What Is Juan Up To?

Mandie was up early the next morning in spite of the fact that she had been up late the night before. Snowball, who usually slept at Mandie's feet, had crawled up the bed, and his purring in her ear woke her.

"Snowball, move," Mandie told the cat as she opened her eyes and found him curled up on her pillow. She gave him a little shove, which brought an angry meow from him as he dug his claws into the bedclothes.

Glancing at her friend, Celia, who was still sleeping, Mandie quietly crawled out of bed, stretched, and went over to the open window for a breath of fresh air. Kneeling down at the low windowsill, she looked out into the early dawn. Faint streaks of light appeared in the east of the gray sky as the sun came up.

"Thank you, Lord, for another day," Mandie murmured as she watched the sky lighten.

She thought of the many mysteries that had appeared during her visit to this old city. She had not been good at solving anything so far. One thing she was sure of was that Bonnie and Ted were the couple she and Celia had seen in the park that night. But how had they known Mandie and Celia would be in the park? She had a feeling they were up to no good, and she was waiting to catch them in their ulterior motives and expose them to her grandmother and Senator Morton.

And who was rearranging their clothes in the wardrobe? And why? It didn't happen every time they left their room, and that in itself was a mystery. Why didn't the person who was doing this change the hangers every time the room was vacated?

"And I just know that was the strange woman from the ship that we saw at the lighthouse," Mandie murmured to herself. "So where is the woman? And what is she doing in St. Augustine? I'd like to talk to her. She might help solve some of these mysteries."

Suddenly Mandie caught a glimpse of two men standing under a palm tree in the yard below. She leaned forward and could just barely see that they were talking as they made gestures with their hands.

"That's Juan!" Mandie exclaimed to herself. "And that is the big man with the beard talking to him." Then she really got excited because she could tell by their motions that Juan was talking to the man! Juan talking! Juan was not really deaf and dumb as everyone thought. She had believed all along that he could talk and hear. So why was he playing deaf and dumb? "Oh, if I could only hear what they are saying!"

Mandie knew that by the time she put on her clothes and slipped downstairs to eavesdrop, the men would probably be gone. But she was going to try anyway. She rushed to pull down her dress from the wardrobe and get into it, then found her shoes nearby. Buttoning the bodice of her dress as she went, she ran down the stairs to the door that led outside beneath her room. Stopping inside to look out through the glass in the door, she saw the two men still in the yard.

"If I open the door, they will probably see me," Mandie moaned in disappointment. "How can I get out unnoticed?" She looked around.

Trying to keep an eye on the men, she glanced around the hallway. There were several windows, but she didn't see another door anywhere. How could she get outside?

Turning back to look through the glass in the door again, she saw the two men shake hands, evidently saying good-bye. Juan started toward the house, and Mandie heard a faint remark from the other man. Juan instantly turned back, and, making motions with his hands, he plainly spoke to the man.

"—meet at the boat . . . tonight . . ." Juan told the man, but Mandie could not hear all his words. To her it sounded like they were making a date to meet at a boat somewhere that evening.

Mandie was so surprised at hearing Juan talk, she almost got caught by him as he entered the house. She dived behind a huge chair nearby, upsetting a lamp, which she grabbed and took down with her as she sat on the floor hidden from his view. She peeked around a corner of the chair and saw Juan look around the hallway. And then to make matters worse, Mandie heard Snowball meow and knew he was not far away. If he came to her, she would be discovered.

Juan stooped down to rub Snowball's head as the cat came up to him. Then the man picked up the cat and set him on the staircase nearby.

"Go! Psst!" Juan told the cat and clapped his hands. Snowball immediately took off running up the steps. Juan laughed and went on down the hallway and disappeared through a door on the left.

Mandie finally let her breath out. She realized she had been holding it ever since Juan came into the house. She quickly rose, set the lamp back on the table, and ran for the stairs.

Mandie made it to her room without anyone seeing her. She stepped inside and closed the door as Snowball dashed in before her. She felt giddy with excitement as she leaned against the closed door.

"Where have you been so early, Mandie?" Celia asked as she rose from the bed and stretched.

"Oh, Celia, you're awake!" Mandie cried excitedly and went to perch on the arm of the chair nearby. "Celia, I was right. Juan can talk. I heard him. He—"

"You heard Juan talk?" Celia interrupted in surprise.

"Yes, he was talking to that big man with the beard we saw before," Mandie tried to explain. "And they made plans to meet at a boat somewhere tonight. I couldn't hear all of it. Oh, Celia, I was right!"

"My goodness, Mandie!" Celia exclaimed. "Where were they? What were you doing? Following them around or what?"

Mandie explained how she had seen them from

the window and had raced downstairs to spy on them.

"I've thought all the time that Juan could hear and talk, and I was right," Mandie declared.

"What are you going to do? Are you going to tell Senator Morton?" Celia asked.

"Probably later, but let's keep this our secret for the time being so we can watch Juan and see what happens next," Mandie told her. "I wish I could have heard where this boat is they are going to meet at, but they were talking so low I couldn't make it all out."

"A boat? Well, at least we know it has to be around water if it's a boat," Celia replied as she got her dress down and began putting it on.

"And there's lots of water around St. Augustine, remember?" Mandie replied. "And there must be lots of boats, too."

"So many that I'd say it's hopeless trying to figure out where they are meeting," Celia agreed.

"Not exactly hopeless, Celia, but hard to do," Mandie told her, sliding back into the chair over the arm. "Now, let me see. We have to plan our strategy." She frowned as she thought about it. "If we watched Juan tonight, we could just follow him when he leaves the house."

"Mandie, you are not talking about roaming around looking for a boat after dark, are you?" Celia asked, brushing her long auburn hair.

"Celia, they said they would meet at the boat tonight, and tonight must mean after dark, I suppose," Mandie replied. "The only problem I see is if Juan decides to leave the house while we are having supper tonight. We can't very well watch him while we eat."

"There's no telling where Juan might go when he leaves the house tonight," Celia reminded her. "Why, we could even get lost following him, and then we'd be in trouble."

"Celia, we couldn't get lost in this town," Mandie protested. "St. Augustine is not that big."

"It's too big for us to go wandering around in after dark, not knowing the streets and everything," Celia said.

Mandie slid out of the chair and stood up. "Celia, are you afraid to go with me?" she asked. "If you are, you don't have to come along. I'm not afraid to go by myself."

"Oh no, Mandie. I couldn't let you go alone," Celia replied, stopping as she tied back her hair. "I'll go with you. I just hope we don't get into any trouble or danger."

"All right, then," Mandie said, walking about the room. "When we see Juan today, we need to watch him and to try and figure out what he's planning. I heard Senator Morton tell Grandmother last night that we would be going to an afternoon tea at his friends' house, and I imagine Juan will go with us since he has been going everywhere else we've gone."

"Afternoon tea?" Celia asked. "Mandie, I hope it's not one of those formal things."

"Me too," Mandie agreed, going over to the bureau and picking up her brush to do her hair. "But I do hope that Bonnie and Ted are there. I'd like to show them up for their underhanded ways."

"On that I agree," Celia replied.

But Bonnie and Ted were not at the tea that afternoon. Mr. and Mrs. John Saylors hosted the tea, and only two other couples besides Senator Morton and Mrs. Taft were invited. The Saylors had a teen-age daughter, Patricia, and an older son, Edward, who were present. They were both friendly but seemed at a loss as to what to say to carry on a conversation with Mandie and Celia, until Mandie asked them a question.

The young people were seated in a corner of the huge parlor, mostly looking at one another, when Mandie suddenly realized the Saylors family had a different accent. Making a guess, she asked the young people, "Y'all don't sound like you come from here. You're not, are you?"

Patricia smiled for the first time and said, "No, we are from New York. We moved down here about a year ago. Everyone notices that we don't speak like the local people."

Mandie smiled back and said, "New York? Oh, I love New York. We have friends up there, and Celia and I have been to visit them. What an exciting time we had!"

"Who are your friends?" Patricia asked.

"Jonathan Guyer. His father is Lindall Guyer," Mandie replied. "And also there's Dr. Plumbley up there. He came from my hometown."

"I have heard the name Lindall Guyer," Edward said, running his long fingers through his black curly hair. "I understand he is very wealthy and contributes to lots of good causes."

"Yes, and no one seems to know where he gets his money or what kind of work he does," Patricia added.

"Oh, I can tell you that—part of it, at least," Mandie said quickly. "Mr. Guyer does secret work for the United States government. And I understand from my grandmother that he owns lots of businesses and things that he inherited."

"Really," Edward said with interest. "Mr. Guyer is a secret agent of some kind. That's very interesting. And that explains a lot of things about rumors I've heard."

"Jonathan stowed away on the ship we took to Europe last year, and we found him," Celia said, smiling at the two.

"Stowed away on a ship? Jonathan Guyer? Why was he doing that?" Edward asked.

"He was running away from boarding school and hoped to make it to his aunt's house in Paris before his father located him," Mandie explained.

Patricia smiled and said, "Let's talk about you two. When are you going back to New York again?"

Mandie and Celia looked at each other and shrugged.

"I don't know exactly, but all of our friends are trying to get something together for the summer where we would visit one another's houses," Mandie explained. "That would include Jonathan's house in New York, and he would come down to North Carolina to my house and the other's homes."

"That sounds like an interesting summer," Patricia said.

"There's only one snag in it," Celia said. "Mandie's friend Joe Woodard is away at college and may have to go to school all summer to get caught up, so we're not sure exactly what we'll do."

"And my mother doesn't like the idea of all of us young people traveling around the country without an adult, so I'm not sure how this plan will work out," Mandie said. Then she asked, "Do y'all know Bonnie Sammons and Ted Tilden?"

"Oh, everybody knows them," Edward said with a big grin.

"Y'all weren't at the masked party at Senator Morton's house, were you?" Celia asked.

"No, we didn't get back from out of town in time for it," Patricia said. "Did you have fun?"

"Well, in a way. But Bonnie and Ted were there, and they seemed a little strange to me," Mandie said.

"You're not the only one who thinks that," Patricia agreed. "Those two don't mix very well with the rest of our society."

Mandie had a sudden idea. "Do y'all know Juan, Senator Morton's servant who can't hear or speak?" she asked.

"Everybody knows of Juan, but few people know him," Edward replied.

"He hasn't been with Senator Morton long, probably a few months, and no one seems to know where he came from," Patricia added. "You know, you would expect the senator to investigate a servant when he hires one, especially since he is a senator and in Washington with the government, but if the senator knows much about Juan, he hasn't told anyone else."

"Oh, Patricia, you know how Senator Morton is," Edward said in a low voice, glancing down the long parlor toward where the senator and the other adults were sitting. "He's always sorry for the downtrodden and will give a person a job on his own evaluation. He seems to be able to judge a person's character pretty well. People he hires stay loyal to him."

"That's what my grandmother said," Mandie

agreed. "But it's too bad Juan can't speak or hear, isn't it?"

"Yes, but he seems to understand everyone and everything all right with hand signs and motions," Patricia replied. "There are lots of different people here in St. Augustine. Why, some of them even believe in ghosts."

"Ghosts?" Mandie quickly repeated. "Yes. Lolly, who works for the senator, definitely believes in them."

"It's not just servants," Patricia told them. "There are some well-to-do people who live in mansions here who claim their homes are haunted by ghosts. Can you imagine?"

"How do they know there are ghosts in their homes? What do the ghosts do?" Celia asked.

"Why, I've heard some people claim lights are turned on and off without anyone being around, and some have heard strange noises, like weeping or fighting," Patricia explained. "And there are some who claim they have actually seen ghosts—that the ghosts appear in person sometimes."

"Do you think you could introduce us to some of these people? I'd love to go into a haunted house," Mandie said with a big grin.

Patricia looked at her in surprise. "You believe in ghosts?" she asked.

"Not exactly," Mandie replied. "I'd just like to talk to people who do. It would be fun trying to explain a mystery that some people think is caused by ghosts."

"Oh, I see," Patricia said with a smile. "Yes, I can arrange for you to meet some of our friends before you leave town."

"Thank you," Mandie replied.

She was really going to get to meet some more people who believed in ghosts. That would be exciting. But right now she began thinking about Juan and the man he was going to meet at a boat somewhere that evening. And she couldn't discuss this with her new friends.

Finally suppertime came at Senator Morton's house. After they were seated in the dining room, Mandie noticed that Juan was staying nearby doing little things to help the servants, like bringing in the coffeepot and making sure their cups stayed filled.

Mandie watched him, and now and then she smiled at Celia. It looked like he was going to stay within their sight at least until supper was over. Then she and Celia would work out the problem of keeping up with him while socializing in the senator's parlor that evening. Maybe Juan wouldn't leave the house until late, after everyone had gone up to bed for the night. But even then it would be hard to watch him because they were supposed to be in their room. She'd figure out something before supper was done with.

Chapter 10 / Business in the Night

Mandie tried to watch Juan when everyone finished their meal and rose from the table that night. As she started to follow Celia and her grandmother and the senator out of the room, Senator Morton said to Mrs. Taft, "Excuse me for a moment. I will catch up with y'all in the parlor. I have a chore for Juan. Be right with you." He walked back into the room.

"Of course, Senator. Come on, girls," Mrs. Taft said.

Mandie glanced back as she went through the doorway and saw Senator Morton standing in front of Juan and making motions with his hands, evidently in an effort to talk to him. *Oh, will the senator be surprised when I finally tell everyone that Juan can hear and talk!* She smiled, anticipating the surprise.

As the girls and Mrs. Taft sat down in the parlor, Mandie did some fast thinking, trying to figure out a way to check on Juan. Glancing at her grand-mother, she asked, "Are we going for a walk?"

Mrs. Taft replied with a loud sigh, "No, dear, I'm just not up to it after all the walking we did today. I'll just sit here with the senator and relax with my cof-fee."

"Would you mind if Celia and I went for a walk, then?" Mandie asked, looking at Celia and then at her grandmother.

"I suppose it would be all right, provided you girls get back in before dark," Mrs. Taft replied. "But, mind you, I did say you must be back inside the house before dark. Remember that."

Mandie quickly rose and motioned for Celia to come with her. "Thank you, Grandmother," she said. "We will get back before dark."

Mandie led the way into the hallway. Celia fol-lowed. Just as they picked up their hats from the hall tree, Senator Morton came toward them.

"Are you young ladies leaving us?" he asked with a big smile.

"Yes, sir. Grandmother gave us permission to go for a walk since she didn't want to go," Mandie ex-plained.

"You really should have someone accompany you," Senator Morton said, pausing nearby. "It won't be dark for quite a while yet, but maybe I should ask Lolly to walk with you."

At first Mandie was going to object, but then she thought it might be helpful to have Lolly along since the girl seemed to know where Juan was all the time. Smiling up at the senator with her blue eyes, Mandie said, "Oh yes, sir, that would be nice. Lolly knows her way around town."

Celia stood there silently listening and shaking

her head behind the senator's back. Mandie couldn't figure out what she was trying to tell her.

"Now, if you two will just wait right here, I'll get Lolly," Senator Morton said, going back down the hallway.

"Mandie, why did you agree to have Lolly come along with us?" Celia asked.

"Because she always knows where Juan is," Mandie whispered. "With a little bit of urging, we can have her looking for Juan."

"But you said Juan was meeting that man tonight, and it's not even dark yet," Celia reminded her.

"I know, but we have to keep up with him until he goes to meet that man," Mandie said. "Otherwise, we'll never know where he is."

Senator Morton came back down the hall with Lolly. "You young ladies have a nice walk, now," he told them and went to the parlor door.

"Yes, sir," the girls chimed together.

"We walk," Lolly said, adjusting a scarf over her long hair.

"Yes, we just want to walk around," Mandie replied.

They went outside and walked toward the park. Mandie stayed alert and glanced back now and then and looked all around, but she didn't see any sign of Juan. Finally she asked Lolly, "Did Juan have to help clean up the dining room?"

"Oh no, no!" Lolly replied emphatically. "Never! Juan no do housework."

"If he doesn't do housework, what does he do?" Mandie asked as they crossed the street.

"What the senator tells him to do," Lolly replied. "Only senator can tell him what to do."

That's interesting, Mandie thought. Juan was not an ordinary servant, then. "What does the senator tell him to do?" she asked.

"Drive carriage, do errands, tend horses," Lolly replied, skipping along, evidently happy at being allowed outside instead of doing housework.

"Horses," Mandie repeated. "I suppose he does have to look after the horses. Come to think of it, where does Senator Morton keep the horses?"

"Stable down road," Lolly pointed off to the right.

"And is the carriage kept there, too?" Celia asked.

"No. Carriage stay in house in backyard," Lolly explained. "Servants live in house in backyard, too."

"They do?" Mandie said in surprise. "I thought they lived upstairs in the big house."

Lolly vigorously shook her head. "Only Juan and Pedro live in big house with senator."

"Pedro?" Mandie said. "I haven't seen him yet. Is he away somewhere right now?"

"No, no," Lolly replied. "Pedro live top floor."

Mandie remembered the man she had seen in the hallway when they first arrived. "Does Pedro not come down to eat or work or anything?" she asked.

"No, Pedro work at church," Lolly said as they walked slowly on. "Pedro live private. Senator make private place for Pedro on top floor."

"Then he must have his own kitchen and everything up there," Celia said.

"What does Pedro do at the church? What kind of work?" Mandie asked.

"Pedro stand up and tell people be good," Lolly tried to explain.

Then he must be a preacher of some kind, Mandie thought. And that was probably Pedro she had seen in the hallway. Mrs. Taft had told them Senator Morton had raised Pedro after his parents died, and he must have educated Pedro also.

"Do you know where Juan is right now? Did Senator Morton send him off on an errand?" Mandie asked as they slowly walked on.

"Yes, Juan go check horses. Senator may go out tonight," Lolly replied.

Mandie stopped to turn and look at her as she asked, "Is Senator Morton going out tonight? I thought he and my grandmother were just going to sit in the parlor and talk and drink coffee."

"Sí, senator go out. Business. Tonight. Late," Lolly replied.

Mandie and Celia looked at each other as they continued down the street.

"Senator Morton goes out on business late at night? Are you sure, Lolly?" Celia asked.

"Sí, senator go out late many times," the girl replied.

"You don't know where he goes, do you?" Mandie asked.

"No, not know that. Juan know. Ask Juan," Lolly said.

Mandie looked at Celia and said in a low murmur, "Maybe we'd better go back to the house and see what goes on there."

"I agree," Celia whispered back.

Mandie looked at Lolly as they went on down the street. She didn't think the girl could have heard the conversation between her and Celia. "Lolly, I think I've walked enough," she said. "Why don't we go back to the house now." She slowed down.

Lolly looked surprised and said, "Tired?" She stopped and sighed loudly. "We go back, then."

They walked back to the house faster than they had left. Mandie was anxious to try to check on Juan. Also, she wanted to be there when Senator Morton left. She wondered if he would speak to her grandmother about where he was going.

Mrs. Taft was surprised to see Mandie and Celia back so soon. She and Senator Morton were sitting in the parlor.

"Y'all weren't gone very long. Is something wrong, Amanda?" Mrs. Taft asked, setting down her cup of coffee on the table by her chair.

"No, ma'am," Mandie replied. "We just decided to come on back and sit down awhile. In fact, I need to see about Snowball. He probably needs to walk around in the yard and get some fresh air. I'll take him out in a little while." She sat next to Celia on a small settee near the senator.

"We did do a lot of walking around town today, so I'm not surprised you two decided to call it quits," Senator Morton said.

After a short while Mandie and Celia went up to their room, got Snowball, and took him out in the yard. They kept watching for Juan but didn't see him anywhere. The evening dragged on, and eventually it was time to go to bed.

"Good night," Mandie told Mrs. Taft and Senator Morton. "I'm going up to my room."

"That's a smart idea," Mrs. Taft agreed. "I'll be doing the same myself shortly. Good night, girls."

But Mandie and Celia had no intention of going to bed when they got in their room. They planned to stay up and watch out the window for anyone going and coming in the yard below.

"I just wonder where Juan went," Mandie remarked as they sat surveying the town below.

Celia suddenly gasped. "Mandie, there is Juan down there! See? He's leaving the yard behind those bushes."

"Come on!" Mandie quickly replied and raced for the door, with Celia following closely.

By the time they got down to the yard, Juan had disappeared, and they walked around in circles in the darkness trying to spot him. Then they saw Lolly suddenly run out of the house and go directly to Juan, who was hidden by a tall bush as he walked away.

"Juan!" the girl called.

Mandie knew he could hear, but he ignored her call and walked on. Lolly finally caught up with him and grabbed his hand. She couldn't hear what Lolly was saying, but Juan shook his hand loose and pointed back to the house for Lolly to go back. He started on his way again, and Lolly finally turned back toward the house.

Mandie and Celia silently circled around to avoid Lolly and then picked up Juan's trail. They followed him directly into the park. He went on through the graveyard there, and they kept following. It seemed to them that he was walking in circles, but he finally made his way down to the dock where they had boarded the ferry for the lighthouse.

Mandie motioned to Celia to stop behind some scrub palmettos that would keep them out of sight. After all the exertion, Mandie's breathing was so fast she was afraid someone would hear her. She heard a faint noise behind her and turned to see Snowball standing there. They must not have closed the door to their room. She grabbed him up in her arms to keep him from meowing.

"Where is Juan going?" Celia whispered, stooping behind the bushes.

"Looks like he's going right into the water," Mandie whispered back.

Juan stopped on the bank and looked around. In a few moments a small boat came to the shore. Two men brought it in and stepped forward to meet Juan.

"Oh shucks! We're too far away to hear what they're saying," Mandie complained.

"There aren't any other bushes nearer where we can move without being seen, Mandie," Celia said.

"Look! One of the men is giving Juan a piece of paper!" Mandie exclaimed in a whisper as she stared into the darkness.

The two men waved good-bye to Juan, went back to their boat, and pushed it out into the water to leave. Juan rolled up the paper, stuck it inside his shirt, and started back.

Mandie and Celia lay down on the ground to keep from being seen. They held their breath and tried to watch Juan through the bushes. Mandie glanced back at the departing boat. There was someone else down there on the bank. She squinted and rubbed her eyes. It was the strange woman from the ship to Europe. *What is she doing here?*

"Look!" Mandie murmured to Celia, who had also spotted the woman.

The woman quickly disappeared behind bushes as she went in the opposite direction of Juan.

Juan came within a few feet of the girls as he strolled on back toward town, evidently not in a hurry. Mandie wished he would hurry past. She wanted to chase after that woman. Finally he got up to the top of the long bank and disappeared.

"Come on," Mandie called excitedly to her friend as she jumped up, ran down the bank, and began searching for the woman. She got to the edge of the water and looked back just in time to see the woman farther down the bank, riding off on a horse.

Mandie finally straightened up as she stopped and stomped her foot. "Oh shucks! They both got away!"

"So we might as well go back to the house now," Celia remarked. "Juan probably walked back that way, but that woman was going in the opposite direction."

"I want to catch up with her," Mandie said impatiently, stomping both her feet as she began walking back toward the road. "Just wait till next time."

The girls returned to the house and went up the outside stairway to their room. They didn't see or hear anyone, and the house was dark except for lamps in the hallway left burning for the night. Pushing open the door to their room, Mandie suddenly realized the door had been completely shut.

"Celia, someone let Snowball out. We did close the door," she told her friend as she set the cat down inside their room.

"If you ask me, there are all kinds of strange things going on around this house," Celia remarked.

Mandie quickly went over to the wardrobe to check their clothes. "No one has bothered our clothes this time," she told her friend.

The girls sat back down at the window to rehash the night's events.

"I'd like to know what that paper was that those

two men gave Juan," Mandie remarked. "And I'd like to know who they are."

"I wonder why they came in a boat like that, in the darkness," Celia said.

"We've just got to figure out what's going on around here with Juan," Mandie said. "He is right in the middle of whatever it is. And especially since he is not really deaf and dumb, I'd say he is guilty of a whole lot of something."

"And I believe Lolly may be involved, too. She seems to be chasing after Juan all the time," Celia added.

"And that strange woman, Miss Wham, she really is here in St. Augustine. I knew that was her we saw at the lighthouse," Mandie said. "I sure can't figure out how she would be connected to anything down here."

"Maybe we can find her somehow," Celia suggested.

"It would be very interesting to be able to find her and ask her questions, wouldn't it?" Mandie agreed.

"We don't know for sure whether she and Juan had contacted each other, or whether one or the other was spying on the other one," Celia remarked.

"And our time here is running out, Celia," Mandie reminded her. "We have to figure out at least part of this puzzle, and soon."

"Mandie, we don't even know where Juan went tonight, or whether he came back to the house or not," Celia remarked.

"I know, but we had to wait for him to get out of the way before we could start back," Mandie agreed. "I just wonder where Lolly's room is here, and whether she might still be up. Let's go investigate."

"This time of night, Mandie?" Celia questioned her.

"Celia, it's not really all that late. Everyone went to bed early. Come on, let's go investigate," Mandie said, going toward the door. "And this time, let's be sure Snowball is shut up in here."

Mandie waited for Celia to go out into the hallway, then she closed the door tightly behind her. Snowball was definitely shut up.

Chapter 11 / Two Men and a Boat

Mandie and Celia slipped back down the outside stairway without seeing or hearing anyone. They crept through the bushes to the backyard and stopped to look up at the small house where the servants lived in the upstairs part. Walking slowly around the building, they couldn't see any lights at all upstairs.

"Everyone must have gone to bed," Mandie whispered.

"And we'd better go back and go to bed ourselves, Mandie," Celia replied.

At that moment there was the sound of horses' hooves and a vehicle entering the front driveway. The girls quickly ducked behind the bushes growing around the house and tried to quietly slip back to the big house to see who was there. They found a space through which they could look into the front yard. Senator Morton was descending from the vehicle.

"Thank you, Pedro," he was saying to the driver. "I'll see you tomorrow." He walked quickly to the front door, and the carriage was driven to the garage behind the house.

"That was Pedro driving and not Juan," Mandie whispered excitedly to Celia.

"Yes," Celia agreed. "That's what Senator Morton called the driver. Mandie, let's go back to our room now."

"We have to wait until Pedro goes in the house or he'll see us," Mandie told her.

The girls waited silently behind the bushes for a long time, watching for Pedro to come out of the garage and go into the house. He never appeared.

Mandie whispered to Celia, "Let's go. Be careful and don't make any noise." She moved forward toward the house. Celia followed.

The girls moved slowly from bush to bush and made their way around to the outside staircase and into the mansion. There was no sign of anyone. They finally reached their room. Snowball was curled up asleep in the middle of the big bed.

Mandie quietly closed the door behind them and blew out her breath. "I wonder where Senator Morton had been," she said, going to the window to look down outside.

"Lolly told us he goes out late at night sometimes," Celia reminded her as she took down her nightclothes from the wardrobe.

"But she said Juan goes with him when he goes out, remember?" Mandie said, bending out the window to look down into the yard. "And that was Pedro driving the carriage tonight." Then she pulled the chair up to the window so she could sit down.

"I know, but I am going to bed, Mandie. It's late,"

Celia told her. She began changing into her night-clothes.

"Good night," Mandie said, watching the yard below.

"Good night," Celia replied as she finished putting on her nightclothes. She crawled into bed, upsetting Snowball, who began meowing and jumped down to join Mandie at the window.

Mandie couldn't see the carriage garage from that side of the house, but she was hoping Pedro would come around there and go up the outside steps to his rooms that Lolly said he had in the top of the house. She wondered why Pedro had driven the senator when Lolly had said it was always Juan who accompanied him when he went out late at night. But then Lolly was probably guessing at a lot of things she had been telling Mandie and Celia. Mandie didn't believe everything the girl had to say.

"Snowball, be still or I'll put you down," Mandie said to the white cat as he tried to curl up in her lap.

Snowball meowed once more and settled down. Mandie's thoughts were jumbled with all the events that had taken place since they had arrived in St. Augustine. Finally she nodded off to sleep in the big chair.

"Mandie!" Celia was calling her name and tapping her on her shoulder. Mandie opened her eyes and looked at her friend. "Mandie, you slept all night in this chair."

Mandie straightened up. Snowball jumped down and ran across the room. She stretched and yawned. "I did?" she asked. "I must have dropped off to sleep while I was watching for Pedro down there." She stood up and stretched again.

"It's almost time for breakfast. You'd better

hurry and get dressed," Celia told her as she went across the room to the wardrobe and took down a dress.

"That was dumb of me," Mandie muttered to herself as she, too, went to find something to put on.

"I overslept," Celia said, hurriedly getting into her clothes. "Mandie, we have been staying up too late since we came down here."

"I know, I know," Mandie agreed as she quickly took off her clothes from the night before and put on a fresh dress. Turning to smile at Celia, she added, "But you know we could always take a nap in the afternoon like Grandmother does sometimes, and then we could stay up later at night."

"Oh no, not me," Celia protested, going over to the bureau to brush her hair.

"Anyway, we'll make it to breakfast on time," Mandie said, looking in the floor-length mirror to check her dress.

The girls did make it on time, but without a minute to spare. As they got to the bottom of the staircase, they saw Mrs. Taft and Senator Morton going through the doorway into the dining room. They rushed in right behind them. Mandie noticed Juan was presiding over the coffeepot again.

As soon as the meal was over, Mrs. Taft told the girls, "The senator and I have some business to attend to in town, Amanda, so you and Celia entertain yourselves while we're gone. We should return by noon."

"Is it all right if we take Snowball for a walk around the neighborhood?" Mandie asked.

"Lolly can go with you young ladies," Senator Morton put in. "I'll tell her."

"Oh no, sir. I mean, we aren't going off anywhere," Mandie quickly said. "We'll stay within sight of the house."

"Well, if you don't go farther than that, it will be all right. But if you decide to go farther away, you'd better ask Lolly to accompany you," Mrs. Taft told Mandie. "Is that understood?"

"Yes, ma'am. I'll remember to ask her if we do," Mandie agreed.

Mrs. Taft and Senator Morton left, and the girls rushed upstairs to get Snowball. Mandie hooked his leash to his collar and carried him down the stairs.

"Aren't you going to feed him before we go out?" Celia asked.

"I suppose," Mandie said, turning down the hall toward the kitchen.

When she pushed open the door, she was surprised to see Juan sitting by a table drinking coffee. Lolly and another maid were moving about the room, stacking dirty dishes for washing, and putting food away.

"Cat need food," Lolly said when she saw the girls with Snowball.

Mandie's mind went to work quickly. Juan had not gone with Senator Morton and her grandmother, so Pedro must have driven the carriage for them. She had to find out why. "No, not right now, Lolly. Would you please just save something for him for later?" Mandie replied, holding on to Snowball, who was trying to get down.

"Sí, miss," Lolly said, putting scraps in a saucer.

"And, Lolly, Senator Morton said we were to ask you to go with us if we went for a long walk. Do you mind going?" Mandie asked, glancing at Juan, who was pretending he had not heard a word she said.

"Now, miss?" Lolly asked, looking up at her.

"If you can go now, that would be fine," Mandie told her. "We'd like to walk all the way across town, so we might be gone for quite a while."

"Un momento, ready in a minute, miss," Lolly said, removing her long white apron and hanging it on a hook by the back door.

Mandie caught Celia's eye and smiled at her. She knew her friend was wondering what she was up to now. Then looking back at Lolly she said, "Lolly, we will meet you back here in about two minutes. We have to go back to our room for something."

"Sí, miss," Lolly agreed.

Mandie and Celia rushed out of the room. They hurried up the steps to their room, and once inside, Mandie closed the door and talked in a low whisper. "Have you figured it all out yet? Juan did not go with the senator, which means he will be around here doing who knows what. I put on the show for his benefit down there. He will think we have left with Lolly and should be gone for a long time. However, when we get far enough away from the house, we are going to park Lolly somewhere and tell her to wait for us. Meanwhile, we will come back to the house and see what Juan is up to."

"But Juan may not be up to anything, Mandie," Celia argued. "And how are we going to get Lolly to just sit and wait for us somewhere?"

"I just feel Juan is up to something or he would have gone with the senator," Mandie said. "And you know Lolly. She likes to loaf. Now come on. Let's go."

Mandie opened the door, stepped into the hallway, and hurried for the stairs, watching as she went for any sign of Juan. Celia followed, and they went back to the kitchen to get Lolly. The maid was ready to go. There was no sign of Juan.

Mandie's plan fell into place easily. After they had walked all the way across the park, Lolly blew out her breath and said, "You walk fast."

Mandie smiled at her, aware that they had been walking very fast, and said, "Lolly, why don't you rest on that bench over there by that shop? Celia and I will just walk around a little more, then we'll come back for you."

Lolly looked at her in surprise. "No want me to walk with you?" she asked.

"Oh yes, we do, but we want you to rest a little," Mandie declared. "Just sit on that bench over there, and we will be right back."

"Sí, I will," Lolly said with a big smile as she walked over to the bench and sat down.

"Wait for us, now," Mandie told her as she and Celia walked on down the street.

"Mandie, what are you up to now?" Celia asked as soon as they were out of Lolly's sight.

"Now we rush back to the house and see what Juan is doing," Mandie told her. "Like I said, he thinks we will be gone a long time. And without Lolly, we can slip back into the house and he won't know it."

"We are going to leave Lolly here?" Celia asked.

"Just for a little while. We can come back and get her," Mandie explained.

"I hope we don't get in some kind of trouble," Celia said.

They hurried back to the house and stayed behind bushes as they made their way to the outside staircase.

"I have to take Snowball back to our room and

shut him up so he won't give us away," Mandie explained in a whisper as they quickly went up the steps.

Once in their room, Mandie said, "I'm going to put him in the bathroom for a little while so we can look around." She started for the door when she happened to glance at Snowball's sandbox in the corner. Someone had brought him a saucer filled with food and placed it there. "He has food. That will keep him quiet." She picked up the saucer and took it into the bathroom. Placing the food nearby, she set Snowball down and he immediately began devouring it. She quickly closed the door.

"Now what?" Celia asked, sitting on the bed.

"We go snoop around and find out where Juan is," Mandie said in a whisper.

Suddenly both girls heard footsteps in the hallway and looked at each other. Whoever it was had paused outside their door.

"Quick!" Mandie whispered, grabbing Celia's hand and diving under the bed. Celia followed.

Mandie held her breath and tried to see the door from under the bed. Her voluminous skirt was twisted around her legs and she couldn't move them, but she managed to slide on her stomach far enough to be out of sight from anyone entering the room. Celia was beside her, gripping her hand. Mandie knew she was frightened.

The girls stayed hidden under there for what seemed like several minutes, and Mandie was beginning to wonder if anyone was coming into the room after all. Then she saw the bottom of the door as it opened silently and a pair of men's shoes entered the room. The door closed slowly, and the shoes walked around the bed.

They're going to the wardrobe, she thought as she twisted around, trying to see. Then she heard the doors to the wardrobe open. Someone was going to rearrange their clothes again. This time she would wait until they were ready to leave the room, then she would crawl out from under the bed in a hurry and catch them.

She could hear the hangers being moved about and waited for the intruder to close the wardrobe doors and leave. Suddenly she realized there was another noise—a strange noise in that direction, a *clickety-click* noise that sounded like—no, it couldn't be. It couldn't. But the noise kept on, and she became confident that whoever it was had a wireless like the one the stationmaster had at the train depot and was busy sending some kind of message. She felt Celia grip her hand tighter and realized Celia had figured it out, too.

But she had moved clothes in and out of the wardrobe several times every day since they had arrived here, and she had not seen a wireless or anything that even resembled a wireless in the wardrobe. So where did this person get the wireless? And why were they using her room to send messages on it? And most importantly, who was doing this, and who was receiving them at the other end? She became a little frightened just thinking about all this. Therefore, when the intruder finished and silently left the room, she didn't move until he was gone.

Finally scrambling out from under the bed, Mandie rushed over to the wardrobe, opened the doors, and looked inside. Celia was right behind her. Their clothes were rearranged again just like before.

"Mandie, that was a wireless," Celia said in a

shaky voice, watching while Mandie pushed the clothes back and forth, searching for the contraption.

"That's what I decided, too, but what would it be doing in our wardrobe?" Mandie said, bending to look inside on the wardrobe floor.

"I kept expecting you to come out from under the bed and confront whoever it was," Celia said.

Mandie straightened up for a moment, looked at her friend, and said, "I was afraid, and it was impossible for us to say our verse, Celia. Whoever it was would have heard us."

"I know, Mandie, but we can say it now, because he might come back and catch us or something," Celia told her, reaching for Mandie's hand.

"You're right," Mandie agreed. Together they recited the Bible verse that helped them in times of trouble. " 'What time I am afraid, I will trust in thee,' " they said.

"Now everything will be all right," Mandie declared and went back to searching the wardrobe.

"Yes, it will," Celia agreed.

Finally Mandie gave up. "There just isn't anything in here that could possibly be a wireless. Everything belongs to us," she declared. "But I am positive that I heard a wireless."

"I am, too, Mandie," Celia agreed. "Maybe it wasn't in the wardrobe but was close by somewhere, in a drawer or something."

"Maybe," Mandie said.

The girls began searching all the furniture in the room and didn't find a thing.

"But why would they rearrange our clothes?" Mandie asked, staring at the tall wardrobe. Then she suddenly said, "Maybe it's on top of the wardrobe."

Both girls reached for the top, but it was too tall for them to touch.

"Let's pull that big chair over here," Mandie said, rushing across the room to tug at a huge chair. "I'll stand up on the back of it. I ought to be able to reach the top of the wardrobe that way."

Celia came to help, and the two finally managed to push the chair in front of the wardrobe. Mandie stood up in it, then stepped onto the arms and thought about stepping up onto the back of the chair, wondering what she could hold on to in order to keep her balance.

Stepping down, Mandie said, "Let's open the doors on the wardrobe, and that way I can hold on to the shelf in the top of the inside if I start to fall."

"Good idea," Celia agreed.

They had to move the heavy chair in order to open the wardrobe doors and then had to push it back. Mandie quickly took off her shoes, then stepped up into the chair and onto the arm. She could barely reach the shelf as she slowly moved up onto the back of the chair. She carefully looked on top of the wardrobe. There was nothing there. Nothing at all.

"Not up here," she told Celia as she slowly stepped down into the chair. She slid on down into the seat and reached for her shoes, which she quickly put back on.

"Mandie, have you forgotten about Lolly? We need to get back to her," Celia reminded her.

"Oh, you're right," Mandie agreed as they pushed the chair back into its proper place.

"Let me just straighten out the hangers with our

clothes, and then I'll be ready to go," Celia said, walking back toward the wardrobe.

"No, no, Celia," Mandie quickly told her. "Leave them the way that person left them. Then if they come back while we're gone, they won't know we've been in here."

"You're right," Celia agreed.

Leaving Snowball in the bathroom, Mandie and Celia crept back down the outside steps and worked their way through the yard behind some bushes until they were clear of the house. Then they hurried back to where they had left Lolly.

When they came within sight of the place, Mandie said, "She's not there!" She rushed on toward the empty bench, looking around as she went.

Mandie and Celia stood there for a minute gazing around the area. Then Lolly came rushing around the corner toward them.

"Si, I am here," she called to them.

"Where have you been, Lolly?" Mandie asked as the girl caught up with them.

"You no come back. I walk," Lolly told her. "I think maybe you no come back at all."

"But, Lolly, I told you we would be back," Mandie said. "I'm sorry we took so long, but we did get back. Now let's go back to the house."

As the three started down the street, Lolly looked at Mandie and then at Celia and said, "White cat. You no have."

"Oh no, we don't have him with us right now," Mandie said, not wanting to tell her they had been back to the house.

However, Lolly had her own explanation. "I wait and I wait," she said. "Then Juan, he come. I tell him you go back toward house and do not come back here—"

"Juan was here?" Mandie interrupted. "You saw Juan?"

"Sí. Juan come from house, go that way for business," she said, pointing off to the left as they walked. "I tell him I wait for you."

"Lolly, if Juan cannot hear or speak, how can you talk to him or he talk to you?" Mandie asked.

Lolly looked confused for a minute, then she said, "We talk with hands and make motions. Juan understand. I understand." She smiled at Mandie.

Mandie didn't believe her and figured Lolly knew Juan could hear and talk all the time. She wondered how Juan managed to keep Lolly from betraying him.

"Mandie, we'd better hurry, remember," Celia said.

"Yes, we have to hurry, Lolly. My grandmother may be back anytime now," Mandie told the girl.

When they got to the house, they didn't see anyone. Lolly headed for the kitchen, and Mandie and Celia went upstairs to their room. They both rushed over to look at the wardrobe. They couldn't see anything different.

"I'd better get Snowball out of the bathroom," Mandie said.

She brought him back to the room, and he immediately jumped on the bed, curled up, and went to sleep.

"So Lolly guessed that we came back to the house and told Juan that we did," Mandie said with a big sigh.

"Do you think it's Juan who has been coming

into our room and going in the wardrobe?" Celia asked.

"I just don't know," Mandie replied. "He would have had to move awfully fast to get done with that wireless we heard and find Lolly way up there where we left her."

"This whole thing is a mixed-up mess," Celia remarked.

"Yes, it is," Mandie agreed. "Even Pedro's involved now. He seems to be driving the senator instead of Juan. And then that strange woman appearing on the beach. Is she in cahoots with Juan, or spying on him? I don't know how we are going to figure all this out, but I think we can if we just keep at it."

Mandie had always been able to figure out mysteries, and she was not going to let this one go unsolved.

Chapter 12 / The Way It Ended

For several days nothing mysterious happened. Patricia Saylors sent a message that she had made an appointment to take Mandie and Celia to visit her friends Mr. and Mrs. Margalosa, who said they had ghosts in their house, if the girls were still interested in going.

Mandie discussed the invitation with Senator Morton and Mrs. Taft at the noontime meal that day. She showed the neatly written note to them and asked, "Would it be all right if Celia and I went?"

"I don't personally know Mr. and Mrs. Margalosa, who own the enormous mansion on the other side of town, but I have heard they claim to have ghosts inhabiting the dwelling with them," Senator Morton said with a smile. "Of course, I do know the Saylors family, where we took you two to visit."

"I really think you should have an adult along with you, Amanda," Mrs. Taft said.

"But, Grandmother, Patricia and her brother Edward will pick us up and then bring us home," Mandie protested.

"I could send Lolly with them if you would like," the senator told Mrs. Taft.

Before she could reply, Mandie shook her head and said, "No, please, Grandmother. We are old enough. We don't need anyone to go with us. Please, Grandmother."

"Well, I suppose it will be all right, provided you go straight there and back, mind you," Mrs. Taft reluctantly agreed.

"Yes, ma'am. Thank you, Grandmother," Mandie said, smiling at Celia.

Mandie was excited as they drove to the Margalosas' mansion, but Celia was a little frightened to be visiting a house where ghosts were said to live. Mrs. Margalosa was an elderly woman dressed in complete black.

"Please come in," Mrs. Margalosa greeted them at the front door. She stepped back and motioned them into a wide, long, dark hallway. "And how are you, Miss Patricia and Mr. Edward?"

They all exchanged greetings, standing there in the hallway. Mrs. Margalosa pointed to a young man at the other end of the hallway. "That is my son, Antonio."

Mandie noticed the son did not speak but quickly disappeared through a doorway back there.

Mrs. Margalosa took them into the parlor where her husband was reading. After she introduced him, they all sat down. Mr. Margalosa had only nodded in their direction.

"Please tell Mandie and Celia about your ghost," Patricia said.

Mrs. Margalosa looked at the two girls, frowned,

and said, "We've been trying to locate him to see what he looks like, but all we get is a steady tapping, and we haven't been able to track that down to its location. But this ghost does make noises sometimes in the middle of the night, which was upsetting until we became used to it. Now we pay it no never mind."

"So you haven't really seen a ghost, then?" Mandie repeated. "Then how do y'all know it is a ghost?"

Mrs. Margalosa looked at her and smiled. "Because we can't find it. Therefore, it must be invisible, which I understand most ghosts are."

"And is it always in the middle of the night when you hear this ghost?" Mandie asked.

"Yes, we've been here nigh on to two years, and we haven't heard it in the daytime at all," the woman said.

"Oh shucks!" Mandie exclaimed. "Then we won't be able to hear it since it's daytime right now."

"You are welcome to come at night, but it's usually late at night that we hear it," Mrs. Margalosa told her.

"We'll have to get permission," Mandie told her.

The four young people prepared to leave. Mrs. Margalosa accompanied them to the front door. They stood in the hallway near the open double doors to the parlor.

"I'm sorry, Mandie." Patricia said. "I didn't realize the ghost can be heard only at night."

"All ghosts creep around in the night," Edward, her brother, teased.

"Then let's get going," Celia suggested.

Mrs. Margalosa opened the heavy front door

while the young people stood there saying good-bye and then stepped outside. Suddenly there was a *tap-tapping* sound from somewhere back in the house.

"Listen!" Mandie cried, turning back.

"Thank you for coming," Mrs. Margalosa said and quickly closed the door in their faces.

The young people looked at one another.

"Did y'all hear that?" Mandie asked.

"Yes," the others agreed.

"Must have been the ghost protesting because we were poking into his business," Edward said with a laugh.

"Do you think we could get back inside the house?" Mandie asked Patricia.

"No," Patricia replied. "You saw Mrs. Margalosa close the door in a hurry. I don't believe she wants anyone investigating her ghost."

The Saylors young people dropped Mandie and Celia back at the senator's house with a promise to see if they could find another place where ghosts lived.

Mandie and Celia went up the outside steps to their room. Mandie had left Snowball closed up and planned to take him out for a walk. There was no sign of anyone else around.

Mandie opened the door to their bedroom and looked around for her white cat. "Snowball, where are you?" she called.

"I don't believe he's here," Celia commented as she helped look.

Suddenly there was a loud noise that sounded like meows and scratching.

"Where is he?" Mandie asked quickly. "The wardrobe. He must be inside the wardrobe." She ran to open the doors to the piece of furniture. Snowball jumped out and ran across the room, meowing and licking his claws.

"How did he get in there?" Celia asked, coming to look.

Mandie surveyed the contents of the wardrobe and said, "Celia, there's something behind our clothes." She quickly began removing the clothes on hangers, and Celia helped.

At last they could see the interior of the wardrobe. On the back side there was a small opening, like a door, standing open. Mandie quickly investigated and gasped at Celia, "There's a wireless inside the wall of the wardrobe. Look!"

"Mandie, I wouldn't touch anything! Senator Morton ought to be told so he can examine whatever it is," Celia cautioned her.

"We didn't imagine things. That was a wireless we heard when we were under the bed," Mandie said. "I wonder what it's doing in there."

"Mandie, let's get Senator Morton," Celia insisted.

Closing the wardrobe door, Mandie turned and quickly left the room with Celia right behind her. They finally located the senator and Mrs. Taft in the parlor. The girls rushed into the room.

"Senator Morton, there's a wireless in our wardrobe!" Mandie told him breathlessly. "And we—"

"A wireless?" Mrs. Taft interrupted.

"A wireless?" the senator repeated. He rose quickly and added, "Would you young ladies please show me what you are talking about?"

Mandie and Celia led the way up the stairs and to their room. Senator Morton followed with Mrs. Taft. The girls rushed across the room to their wardrobe and flung open the doors.

"In there! In that secret panel at the back," Mandie told him as she moved so he could look inside.

"Where, Miss Amanda? I don't see anything like that," Senator Morton replied.

Mandie and Celia both crowded forward to look into the wardrobe. The wireless was gone! The secret compartment was empty.

"It was here, Senator Morton. I saw it with my own two eyes," Mandie insisted.

"I did, too," Celia added.

"Then what happened to it?" Senator Morton asked, bending inside the piece of furniture to examine the compartment. "I don't see any sign of it."

"Somebody must have heard us when we found it, or when we told you," Mandie said. "But it really and truly was there. We both saw it. And we also heard it the other day." She explained about crawling under the bed that day.

Mrs. Taft looked at Senator Morton and said, "You must have some dishonest people around here."

Then Mandie remembered hearing the sound at Mrs. Margalosa's house and told the senator about that.

"Seems there's a lot going on around here," the senator said thoughtfully. "Don't you young ladies worry about this. I'll look into everything and take care of it."

Mandie could see the senator did not intend discussing any suspicions with her, or giving any explanations if he was aware of the setup. He and Mrs. Taft went back to the parlor. The girls went outside to walk Snowball around the garden.

"Senator Morton didn't seem very interested in

the fact that someone had put a wireless in that wardrobe, did he?" Mandie remarked as she held on to Snowball's red leash.

"He might not have believed us, Mandie," Celia told her.

"I think he believed us, but that he also knew about it," Mandie said.

"Knew about it?" Celia repeated.

"Yes, it must have been some kind of setup he had for some reason or other," Mandie said thoughtfully.

"Do you mean you think it was Senator Morton who has been coming in our room and going into the wardrobe to use that wireless?" Celia asked.

"Maybe," Mandie replied. Snowball jumped after a butterfly in a bush and almost jerked the leash out of her hand. "Snowball, leave that pretty butterfly alone." She tightened her grip to pull him back. "Anyhow, I am going to watch Juan every minute that I can. He may be the one. After all, he is pretending he can't speak or hear."

Although the girls were on the lookout for Juan after that, they didn't see him again for two days. They were again in the yard when he suddenly rushed through the shrubbery from the carriage house in the backyard and into the back door of the house. They tried to follow, but he was too quick, and they were unable to tell where he had gone.

That same night Mandie and Celia were sitting in their window before going to bed and saw Juan below in the front yard.

"Look, that's Juan down there," Mandie said. "Let's go down and watch him." She raced for the door, and Celia came right behind her.

The moon was shining brightly, and the girls

slowed down outside to keep within the shadows of bushes and trees as they made their way toward the spot they had seen Juan.

"There!" Mandie whispered in Celia's ear, pointing ahead. Juan was standing in the shadows next to the trunk of a large palm tree.

The girls quickly darted behind another tree to watch the man. Almost immediately another figure came up to Juan in the dark. Mandie gasped to herself when she realized it was none other than the strange woman, Miss Lucretia Wham. Her heartbeat quickened as she grasped Celia's hand and tried to listen. Miss Wham was speaking rapidly to Juan, and he seemed to be hearing what she was saying.

"—Margalosa . . . Antonio . . ." were about the only words Mandie could make out. Miss Wham was talking about the Margalosas for some reason.

Then Juan straightened up and said plainly, "They have all been taken in by the marshal tonight."

"Then I will return to Washington tomorrow," Miss Wham said.

Mandie was itching to run out from her cover and speak to the woman, but for some reason she was afraid to, and she wanted to make sure she heard everything she could.

"I will tell the senator immediately," Juan replied.

At that moment there was the sound of footsteps near them, and Mandie cautiously looked behind her and saw Lolly rushing through the yard toward Juan. When she looked back at Juan, the strange woman had disappeared and he was alone. He must have seen Lolly approaching because he did not seem surprised that she was there when she came up to him.

"Get your things ready. We leave before daylight tomorrow," Juan told the girl.

"Then we have accomplished what we came for," Lolly said in an educated voice, surprising Mandie. The girl must have been posing as a maid and was not really one after all.

"Yes, I am going now to inform the senator. Be ready before the sun comes up," Juan said, walking toward the house.

"Yes, sir. I'll be waiting for you," Lolly said, and she walked off toward the back of the house, where she lived in the upstairs of the carriage house.

Mandie stood there completely confused. *What was going on?* Lolly was not really a maid, and Juan was some kind of partner with her. Could it be that those two had set up the wireless for some crooked reason, and now that Mandie and Celia had discovered it, they had decided to move on out of town?

"Let's go," Celia urged Mandie.

"This is strange," Mandie whispered as she and Celia carefully made their way back to the outside steps.

Once back in their room, the girls tried to figure out the mystery. Mandie sat down near the window to watch below again. Celia began getting ready for bed.

"What do you think that was all about, Mandie?" Celia asked, taking down her nightclothes from the wardrobe.

"Well, to begin with, I believe Senator Morton knew all the time about the wireless," Mandie replied. "And there must be something going on between Juan and Lolly. And Miss Wham is involved in all this. It sounded to me like the Margalosas are in trouble of some kind."

"Yes, I agree," Celia said, putting on her night-clothes and then going over to sit by Mandie. "Aren't you going to get ready for bed?"

"No, because I want to watch for Lolly and Juan when they meet before daylight like they planned," Mandie replied. Looking at her friend, she asked, "Did you hear Miss Wham say she was returning to Washington tomorrow?"

"Yes, I did," Celia replied. "And, Mandie, I figure she is still working for the president or at least for the government, don't you believe?"

"That is exactly what I thought, too," Mandie agreed. "But I wonder what it could be about."

"I see someone else down there, over to the left . . . under that huge tree," Celia told Mandie.

Mandie quickly squinted and leaned out the window. "Yes, there are two men down there!" she exclaimed. "I am going back downstairs." She raced for the door.

"Soon as I get my dress back on, I'll come, too," Celia called to Mandie as she went out the door.

As Mandie reached the yard, a fire ignited over in the front corner. The bushes and trees seemed to be burning. Mandie kept running toward it to see what was happening. The two men were nowhere in sight, and they had evidently set the fire. Turning back to the house, she started screaming as loudly as she could, "Fire! Fire! Come quick, somebody. Fire!" She ran as fast as her wobbly, frightened legs would take her and almost collided with Juan as she opened the front door. He was rushing outside.

"Why do you scream?" Juan asked, putting out a hand to stop Mandie.

"Fire! Fire! Out there!" Mandie gasped for breath as she pointed.

Juan immediately raced outside with Mandie following. When he saw the fire, he called to her, "Wake everyone! Call Lolly, call Pedro, all the servants. Quick!" He ran out toward the fire.

Mandie reentered the house, screaming as she rushed toward the kitchen, not knowing where to find the servants at this hour of the night. When she pushed the door open, she found Lolly drinking a cup of coffee by the stove. Lolly looked up at her in alarm.

"Fire in the front yard! Juan said call everyone to help!" Mandie cried with her last breath as she collapsed into a chair.

Lolly handed Mandie her cup of coffee and turned to leave the room. "Drink this!" she exclaimed as she ran to the door.

Mandie took a swallow of the hot liquid, set it down, and ran for the stairs. Her grandmother was asleep upstairs, and the fire could spread to the house. Reaching her grandmother's room, Mandie didn't bother to knock. She opened the door and went to wake Mrs. Taft, who was already sitting up.

"Grandmother, get dressed. The front yard is on fire," Mandie told her. "I have to get Snowball and Celia." She quickly left the room and ran on to her room.

Celia had heard the screaming and was fastening on Snowball's leash when Mandie got there. "Is it bad?" Celia asked as she handed the white cat to Mandie.

"It will probably spread if they don't get it out

real fast," Mandie told her, cuddling Snowball in her arms.

As the girls rushed back down to the yard, Mandie told Celia what had happened. "I saw two men, and they disappeared. I believe they were the men Juan met at the boat," she said between breaths.

When they came down into the yard, all the servants were fighting the fire as Senator Morton shouted orders. When he saw the two girls, he called to them, "Stay back. We can handle this, and y'all might get hurt."

"Yes, sir," Mandie replied, and turning to Celia, she said, "Snowball is afraid. Would you mind holding him and walking back toward the house away from the fire? I have to help, no matter what the senator says." She held out her cat.

Celia took Snowball and tried to calm him. "Mandie, he told us to stay away," she reminded Mandie as she slowly backtracked toward the house.

"I know. I'll catch up with you in a little bit," Mandie replied. She rushed toward the fire on the side away from the senator. The servants had large pieces of carpetlike material that they were beating at the fire with. She grabbed up an extra piece from the pile nearby and began helping.

It was a tough job, but after a while the people were able to smother out the last remnants of the fire. They had kept it from progressing toward the house. Everyone paused for a breath, and Mandie looked around the group. She saw her grandmother standing in the background with Celia. Senator Morton, tired and dirty, started toward Mrs. Taft. Mandie quickly put out a sooty hand to detain him.

"Senator Morton, I think I know who set the

fire," Mandie told him. "Juan met two men in a boat one night, and I believe that's who did this. I saw two men in the dark, and it looked like them."

"Yes, that is what we figured," Senator Morton said. "I thank you for sounding the alarm before it got completely out of control."

"If you really want to thank me, would you please explain what is going on?" Mandie replied, looking up at the senator with her blue eyes in a sooty face. "Celia and I have been watching and listening, and we think we have it all figured out. Would you please tell me what has been happening since we came?"

"I suppose it is no longer secret information," the senator replied after a long pause. "There has been smuggling going on down on our coast—boats from Cuba, which makes it a federal case. Juan works for me in my Washington office, and when I was asked to investigate, I brought Juan down here. Then Miss Lucretia Wham, whom you previously knew, appeared, apparently sent down by the president himself. Juan had set up the wireless in your wardrobe to keep in touch with other government people, and your room was not supposed to be occupied. But when the maid put y'all in there, I figured it would be all right." He stopped to smile at her.

"What about the Margalosas?" Mandie asked. "I heard some conversation regarding them."

"Yes, they are involved. They were trying to intercept Juan's messages," the senator explained. "They were picked up by federal agents last night."

"And Lolly? She is not really a maid, is she?" Mandie asked.

Senator Morton smiled and said, "I do believe

you would make a good agent for the government when you grow up, Miss Amanda. No, Lolly actually works for Miss Wham."

"Oh, I see," Mandie replied. "And when Celia and I found the wireless in our wardrobe, that started things moving faster."

"Yes, ma'am," he agreed. "Now that you know, do you mind if I join your grandmother over there to see if she is all right?"

"Oh, thank you, Senator Morton," Mandie replied. "I thank you for helping me solve the mystery." She smiled at him and started toward Celia.

Mandie raced over to Celia to share the information. They discussed it as they started toward the outside stairs. It was still nighttime, so the girls cleaned up and got in bed and continued their conversation into the wee hours of the morning.

The next morning at the breakfast table, Mrs. Taft told Mandie, "You and Celia should get dressed when we finish our food. We are going to visit the Saylors family again."

Mandie looked at her in surprise, and then down at the perfectly good dress she was wearing. "But, Grandmother, I am dressed," she said. "This is a nice dress."

"Let's just put on something more dressy," Mrs. Taft insisted.

Mandie looked at Celia, who was smiling, and said, "I suppose that includes you, too."

"Yes," Celia agreed.

Mandie wondered why they were visiting the Saylorses in the morning. Visits were usually made in the afternoon or at night. Oh well, her grandmother came up with her own ideas sometimes. And Mandie looked forward to relating the events of the night before to Patricia and Edward. Senator Morton had said she could talk about the mystery now that it was solved.

Patricia and Edward were expecting the girls, and Mandie was surprised to see that they were also dressed in what she liked to call their "Sunday-go-to-meeting" clothes.

"So you saved the house from the fire," Edward said with a big grin for Mandie.

"Well, I don't know about that, but I saw those two men down there, and, of course, I figured they were up to no good," Mandie replied.

"But I heard that you actually got out with the servants and helped extinguish the fire. That was very brave of you, Mandie," Patricia told her.

"Not really. I didn't stop to think about danger or anything. I just knew I didn't want Senator Morton's house to catch on fire," Mandie said with a shrug. She was always uncomfortable with compliments.

The conversation centered around the fire for the next hour, and then Senator Morton spoke from across the room. "Those are two brave young ladies. They even helped track down lawbreakers for the federal government." Looking at Mandie, he added, "It's all right if you would like to tell your friends about it. The case is wound up and closed."

"Oh, thank you, Senator," Mandie replied. She immediately went into a fast account of finding the wireless and seeing the two men in a boat.

"How exciting!" Patricia exclaimed.

"And also dangerous," Celia added.

"It certainly is dangerous to snoop into things like that. I'm so glad you two girls came out unscathed," Edward told them.

Mandie noticed for the first time that Edward was evidently trying to flirt with her. He was good-looking and seemed to have a friendly personality, but he couldn't compare with Joe Woodard. And she wished she could see Joe to relate all these adventures she and Celia had been having since they came to St. Augustine. She thought about home.

Mandie was suddenly aware that her grandmother had risen and was speaking to her. "Amanda, I think we will be returning to Senator Morton's now."

Mandie stood up quickly. "Oh yes, ma'am." She turned to Patricia and Edward and said, "I'm so glad I got to know y'all, and I hope y'all will come visit me sometime."

"Oh yes, we will," Patricia promised.

"Soon," Edward added with a smile.

Since Juan had left for Washington that morning, Pedro was now driving the senator's carriage. He pulled up in front of Senator Morton's house, and everyone stepped down.

"Amanda, let's just go in the parlor for a minute before you girls go upstairs to your room, or wherever you are headed," Mrs. Taft told her.

Mandie looked at her grandmother, wondering why, and said, "Yes, Grandmother."

When the girls and Mrs. Taft and Senator Morton stepped into the front hallway, Mandie noticed the door to the parlor was closed. The senator reached forward to open it, remarking, "Now I just wonder who closed this door." He flung the double doors wide.

Mandie stood there frozen with surprise, while shouts of "Happy Birthday!" came from within the parlor. There were her friends, every one of them, she decided as she looked around. Tears of joy began streaming from her blue eyes. She had forgotten today was her birthday, but her friends had not.

Uncle Ned, her father's old Cherokee friend, stepped forward, put his arm around her, and led her into the room. "Happy birthday, Papoose," he said.

Mandie turned, buried her face on his shoulder, and cried uncontrollably.

Then Joe was tugging at her hand, "Come on, crybaby," he said, "We've got chocolate cake."

Sallie, Dimar, Jonathan, and Morning Star crowded around her. Mandie turned to look at them and spied her mother and Uncle John in the far corner, smiling and watching the greetings. Mandie broke loose and ran to her mother.

Elizabeth squeezed her daughter in her arms. "This is such a special day. Fourteen years ago you were born, my dearest darling," she said.

"Oh, Mother, I love you so much," Mandie said in a shaky voice, and reaching to hold Uncle John's hand, she added, "You, too, Uncle John."

The party began. Mandie and her friends talked nonstop the rest of the day. Then Mandie learned they would all be staying that night with the senator, and the next day everyone, including her and Celia, would be going home.

"Yes, we need to get back and see what's going on at home," Mrs. Taft said.

"And if there's not a mystery there, Mandie will find one," Joe said, squeezing her hand. He bent to whisper in her ear, "I love you, Mandie Shaw."

Mandie felt her face turn red, and she looked around. Evidently no one else had heard that remark. Then looking up at the tall boy, she said, "I've missed you, Joe Woodard."

The two looked at each other and smiled. Mandie felt her heartbeat quicken and her hand shake a little as it was held by Joe Woodard. There were lots of things ahead for the summer, and Joe had actually made it home from school.

Great Gifts for MANDIE

The **MANDIE Datebook** is a reminder of birthdays and other important dates. Highlights occasions Mandie holds dear! Hardcover.

The **MANDIE Diary** is a perfect place to write special thoughts. Features a brass lock and key! Hardcover.

SNOWBALL Stationery is the purr-fect way to write letters to friends—or fan letters to author Lois Gladys Leppard! Timesaving tri-fold stationery includes self-adhesive stickers to seal notes-no envelopes needed. Set of 12 notes and stickers.